Thread and **THRUM**

Jane Bower

CW00535959

Thread and THRUM

A novel for children
and their grown-ups

Jane Bower

Illustrated by
Len Bower

 **Epic Ink**

Dedicated to the children of Strone, Yanwath,
and Caton Primary Schools,
and the memory of our magical story times
1974-1987

First published 2020

Epic Ink is an imprint of
Epic Storytelling Ltd
43 Norfolk Road, Wyton
Huntingdon, Cambridgeshire PE28 2EF

© Jane Bower, 2020
Illustrations © Leonard Bower, 2020

The right of Jane Bower to be identified as the Author
of this work has been asserted in accordance
with the Copyright, Designs and Patents Act 1988.

All rights reserved. No part of this book may be reprinted
or reproduced or utilised in any form or by any electronic,
mechanical or other means, now known or hereafter invented,
including photocopying and recording, or in any information
storage or retrieval system, without the permission in writing
from the Publishers.

British Library Cataloguing in Publication Data.
A catalogue record for this book is available from the British Library.

ISBN 978-1-9997523-2-3

Typesetting and origination by Epic Ink
Printed in Great Britain

CONTENTS

THANK YOUS

I wrote this book in celebration of my father – an artist who, despite losing his sight, has gone on to lead a life full of interest and appreciation. It is in honour of him that 30% from the sale this book will go to the Macular Society.

The book is also for my mother, who first introduced me to the wonders of words and stories by reading to me every single night, right into my teens —one of the most valuable gifts a parent can give.

It is thanks to the input of both my parents that I went on to become a teacher, writer, artist, and performer, travelling to primary schools throughout the UK and beyond, and leading workshops in art, drama, dance, and storytelling.

My grateful thanks are also due to Chip Colquhoun of Epic Ink, whose meticulous and caring suggestions and guidance I have respected and valued enormously; Joan Nixon, former secretary of Caton School, who typed out in her own time the very first draft of the book; and to Revd Cristina Cipriani and Dr Simone Maghenzani for help with the Venerable Bead's Italian phrases.

– Jane Bower, December 2020

PROLOGUE:
LOSING THE THREAD

She really did break the thread quite viciously.

It is strange how good things come out of bad things. A bad temper is not a good thing. But if that particular girl hadn't had one that particular day and pulled that particular necklace apart, the story – and all stories have a thread – wouldn't have started at all.

What the temper was about, she has quite forgotten – so she claims.

When the necklace was broken, its many beads fell dazed to the floor and rolled and rumbled helplessly towards the corners. Most of them, as time passed, were removed one way or another – though what happened to them is not at all clear. What *is* clear is that one bead remained unconscious in a corner for a long time – and when he came round, he could see none of his companions on the whole surface of the vast floor, and it seemed that no-one could see him either.

He tried to roll, but he was too bruised. He had managed to lodge in one of those places which people rarely investigate, behind a wooden cabinet, which to the poor bead seemed to stretch upwards into infinity. Day after day he lay, and it seemed he was doomed to lie there forever, until a moment came when something – everything – was changed.

The bead was lying in his cold, hard corner, hoping. He hoped for most of the day now, but so far it hadn't done much good. He was passing the time in hope when a shadow was cast over him – and as he looked up, the whole solid wall of the cabinet lurched and scraped aside. In terror the bead stared as a huge, claw-like, pendulous shape descended from above, two of its fleshy, soft pincers poised to winkle him out of his corner like a snail from its shell.

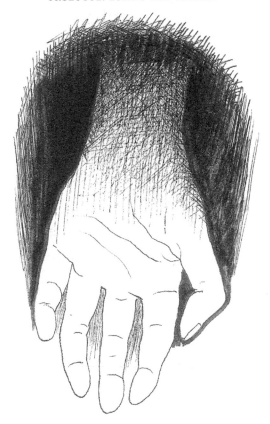

The bead squeaked in panic – but beads, like bats, make sounds inaudible to human ears, so he was not heard. He only felt himself suffocating as he was enclosed in podgy pinkness and rolled sickeningly backwards and forwards, being inspected. After long minutes of being swung mercilessly up and down, he was dropped from a great height, in a state of total desperation, into a large walled arena and onto a hard, bobbly surface.

With a clangorous grating, his world went suddenly dark.

When the bead had stopped shaking and had realised that all was silent, he dared to open his eyes. It took time for them to adjust. But then, in a faint shaft of greyish light from above, he saw around him dozens of other pairs of eyes. Rigid with fear, the bead started suddenly as he heard a slightly scornful voice.

"He looks terrified." The words seemed to emanate from a toffee-coloured sphere in the gloom. "Better start getting used to it. We're all in the same boat here."

"B-boat?" questioned the stricken bead. Was he at sea?

There was a murmur of derisive laughter as a kinder voice explained:

"He means we're all in the same situation. You're one of us now. You're in the Bead Box."

"Am I?" the bead asked, hopelessly. He wanted to cry.

The first voice replied. "Course you are. The Hand

just dropped you in and shut the lid. Stop cowering and let's have a look at you."

Uneasily, the bead allowed himself to be examined. He took a cautious look at his examiners from the corners of his eyes. Most of them were bigger than he was, and looked more confident. Some were brightly coloured or carved. He knew he did not present a very impressive picture.

"Hmm," said a larger, reddish bead in a Cockney accent. "Not exactly from the Queen's tiara, are yer?"

It was true. The bead was small and round and brown. He was made of wood which had once been highly polished but was now somewhat dull.

He knew that there were probably thousands of other beads who looked just like him and that he would never be anyone special. But he had good wood grain; he had once heard a friend of his owner say so.

"What's your name, Big Ears?" said the Cockney bead, who had once been geometrical in shape but who now had very worn edges.

The small bead blushed under his brown polish. He knew that his ears were big.

Beads' ears are the holes through their middles. Some beads have tiny delicate ears that are too small for anything but the finest silk. Beads can hear slightly better when they are not strung. Since the cord goes in one ear and out the other, their hearing can be muffled when on a necklace – though most beads find this a cosy sensation, like being cocooned in cotton wool, and it brings them contentment. It is important to choose the correct cord – a smooth cord, narrower than the ears – so that the beads can move freely, and are not scratched or deafened.

But the bead could hear now. He could hear a steady background noise, a permanent, reverberating sound, which had been there since he arrived. He longed to be back on his comforting thread. His ears were large and crude – big enough to put string through, he thought balefully – and he was being teased about them.

"I haven't got a name," he stammered, his lip quivering. (Oh yes, he had a mouth. Beads have mouths, but they are only for talking. They do not need to eat; they just last until they wear out.)

"Well, you ought to 'ave. You look like a plum puddin'," the red Cockney bead said, poking him – though not hard.

"Says about as much as a pudding as well," added a sour yellow bead with stripes.

"The Wooden Pudden!" shouted the red bead, and it seemed that they all rolled and roared and wheezed, leaving the poor brown bead sitting in the middle of them feeling worse than he had ever felt in his life.

Taking no more notice of him, the larger beads pushed and jostled off further into the Bead Box. A quietness returned, though the ever-present vibration continued, and blackness closed in like the blackness of a coffin.

The bead sat solitary, and to look at him it would have been impossible to guess at the turbulent emotions inside him. His quivering lip was hardly visible, and neither were his eyes.

There are many ways to disguise a bead's eyes and mouth: in the centres of dots or flowers, in a carved design or a painted pattern. This bead's features were in the knots of his wood.

But it is not so easy to disguise tears – and, since beads have no arms or legs, it is not at all easy to wipe them away. The bead's tears dropped silently down his wooden surface – and he sat, lost among innumerable strangers.

That night, he stopped hoping.

CHAPTER I:
NAMING NAMES

He must have sunk into a weak sleep, for he woke with a forceful jolt into an immediate state of terror.

It seemed to be still night, yet the bead's large, round ears were absorbing the same steady noise level which suggested it was day. His own uncertainty terrified him more, and he sat exactly where he was – desperate for something to happen which would explain everything, yet fearing any new occurrence.

A voice behind him made him turn for the first time.

"Good afternoon."

"A– afternoon?" repeated the little bead blankly. "I thought... It seemed like night."

"It's just that you're not used to the dark," continued the voice, and the little bead recognised it as the kind one belonging to the bead who first told him he was in the Bead Box. "It's always dark in here. But it's actually afternoon."

The friendliness of the voice relaxed the little bead somewhat, and he ventured to ask, "How do you know?"

"The Crack," came the reply.

The little bead gave up. He had, for one moment, thought that he was going to make some sense out of this terrible new existence, but he knew now that there was no hope. He couldn't understand any of it – boxes and boats and puddings and cracks – and he was certain he never would. Tears formed miniature twin beads in his bead eyes and he turned mournfully away.

"Oh, come on, little chap, don't get in such a state!" The voice sounded faintly amazed at the little bead's reaction. "Turn round again."

A stifled sob was the little bead's only response. There was a short silence.

"OK; if you won't turn round to me, I'll have to come round to your side."

Cautiously the tearful bead peeped from his eye corners. He heard a light rolling noise, and there in front of him stood the new bead – slightly larger than himself, and a pleasant blue in colour. There was nothing particularly special about him except that he had a remarkably clear, smooth, and beautiful surface. You noticed this if you took the trouble to look. But otherwise he was just an ordinary, medium-sized blue bead.

Again there was silence.

"Would you like me to tell you what The Crack is?"

The small brown bead gave an indefinable squeak.

The blue bead sighed. "Look," he said, "I really needn't bother you. I could just go away and leave you. But I've seen a few newcomers here in my time, and none of them has sat weeping and rigid with fear well into the night and then had bad dreams till the following afternoon. You can muck in like the others and learn the hard way or I can give you a few tips now. I'll leave you to decide and you can come and find me if you want me."

"No." It was the first decisive word the little bead had spoken since his arrival. He pulled himself up a little straighter. "Tell me about The Crack, please."

The blue bead looked hard at the small, round figure in front of him.

"Right," he said. "The Crack is where the lid of the Bead Box doesn't fit properly. It's our way of telling what time of day it is. When light starts coming through, we know it's morning. You won't be able to tell for a while, but then you will. Seems dark to you, doesn't it?"

"Oh yes." The little bead thought he had never seen such darkness in daytime.

"Well, this to me is quite light. It's what you get used to. I travelled up to The Crack once. It was a rough climb, because the Highs don't like you pushing them down, but I wanted to see what it was like."

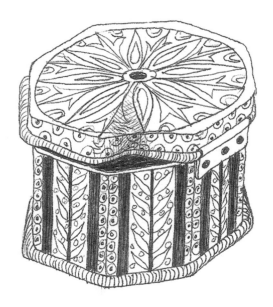

"What was it like?" the young bead asked. He was more anxious to hear news of the outside world than to know who the Highs were.

"Oh..."

The blue bead's voice took on a distant sound, and it seemed to the listening bead that it was tinged with sadness. Then it continued briskly.

"I'm sure I needn't tell you. We've all been Outside, after all."

The little bead instinctively felt that he should not pursue this theme any further. Instead he asked, "Have you a name?"

"Yep. Pebble," the blue bead said. He bounced up

and down once or twice, slightly self-conscious. Then he added, "Look... I'm sorry you got called... what you got called earlier."

The small brown bead shrugged. He hadn't minded that much, as he sensed the red bead had probably meant it to be a bit of a joke – even though it wasn't very funny – and besides, he didn't have another name. He looked in awe at the smooth body and enviable colour of his companion. It must be wonderful to be smooth and blue and have a real name like Pebble, and climb all the way up to The Crack and know about things.

"Tell me some more about the Bead Box, please, Pebble," he said huskily.

"What do you want to know? First and most, I mean."

"Well – who those other beads were last night, and what the sound is, and when I can go home, and..."

He stopped because Pebble was looking at him with patient pity, and his mouth was firmly compressed.

"I will go home, won't I?" the small bead said in sudden panic.

Pebble's expression did not change.

"Pebble, tell me, speak to me, why are you looking like that? Pebble, *please...*"

"There's a lot you don't understand," Pebble said quietly. Then his tone became brisk again. "Let's talk about those other fellows you met last night."

The bead wasn't entirely satisfied – and wasn't sure that "fellows" was how he would describe them – but he listened meekly, as he was curious.

"The first one that spoke to you, said you looked terrified – remember?"

The little bead nodded. He remembered the toffee-coloured bead all too well.

"Well, that was Amber. He's always the first in a crowd. Fancies himself as a bit of a leader. Don't let him get to you. He puts on the airs and graces. Tries to make out he's the real stuff, too."

"Real stuff?"

"Amber. He's the right colour, of course – always fools a few, but most of us know better. We say Amber's a good name for him because you can see right through him." He chuckled a little.

"What – what is he, then?" the young bead asked.

Pebble looked to the left and the right, and then leaned forward to one of the smaller bead's dark hollow ears.

"Plastic," he hissed. "One hundred percent. Not that I mind," he went on genially, "it's all the same to me. I felt quite sorry for him when I found out."

"How did you find out?" the little bead whispered, wide-eyed.

Pebble moved nearer once again. "Hong Kong," he mouthed breathily. "He leaned over once, didn't know I was watching. There it was. Stamped all over his – er..."

He jerked his eyes over his own back.

"...derrière."

"Derry– oh," the small bead said, realising. He wasn't sure whether to laugh or be shocked.

"Exactly," the blue bead resumed. "It's the bane of his life. That's why he shuffles along like that, to hide it. Lives in horror of anyone finding out."

The little bead was amazed. He had never pretended to be anything but wood. He tried to imagine living his life like Amber, but couldn't.

"Then there was old salad features, the yellow-coloured one with the green stripes. That's Mellow. She doesn't use many kind words, I'm afraid, that one. Always sniffing and looking superior. Sad, really." Pebble gave a sigh and looked resigned.

"Mellow?" the small bead repeated. It was not a word he used often, but he thought it meant calm, relaxing, mature. It didn't seem to fit the character of the bead he had encountered.

"Oh – well, Melon actually," Pebble said, with a quick grimace. "She changed it – not too happy with it, I gather. Rhymes with yellow, so she makes out that's why it's her name."

The brown bead nodded slowly. As a name, Melon made much more sense – but he could see that Mellow might be preferable. So she was hiding the truth too.

"Then, I think the only other one who spoke to you was Rough."

The beadling guessed that this must be the large Cockney who had made him feel slightly afraid. Something about the memory must have shown in his expression, because Pebble said:

"I can understand if you found him off-putting, but he's good-hearted underneath. You've got the right one, haven't you? Big, red fellow. Came up from London years ago. He's so worn now, he knows he'll never be Chosen. Used to be a diamond shape, with straight edges – quite handsome really. If you look hard, you can imagine what he would have looked like when he was younger. That's where he got his name, of course. Rough Diamond, his full name is."

There was silence as the little bead digested this information. Then something Pebble had said set the old fears creeping back, slowly at first, then with gathering speed.

"What about my other question, Pebble?" he said. "You asked what I wanted to know most, and –"

Pebble sighed. "OK, OK," he said. "You'll have to know anyway. It's about going home, isn't it?"

The bead nodded urgently.

Pebble sighed again, as if he didn't know quite how to begin. "The point is this," he said. "It's like Amber told you. We're all in the same boat – that means the same circumstances. We all came from our various places: necklaces, bracelets, whatever. We've all ended up here. And – well, to be blunt, until the Hand comes, here we stay."

There was a rigid silence. Pebble stared downwards. Slowly the little bead grasped the meaning of his words. It was as if a liquid, something deadly, was seeping, penetrating his wood, reaching its very heart and threatening to crack open the grain. He understood.

Pebble half-coughed, half-choked awkwardly, aware of the effect of his words. "It's always unpleasant to break it to new arrivals," he said, "but you've taken it well. Anyway," he went on, endeavouring to sound bright, "we can't complain at our chances. We're Upper Middles."

The bead could not yet speak, but stared questioningly.

"We're among the middle layers of beads in the Box," Pebble explained. "I told you the Highs don't like you altering their position. They're on the top, see? If the Hand opens the lid, they'll be seen first, so they've most chance of being Chosen. But Upper Middle's not bad."

The bead found his voice. "Do you mean... there are layers and layers of beads like us, underneath us at this very moment?" he asked incredulously.

"Oh, yes," Pebble said, as if it was the most ordinary thing in the world. "That's the thrum you can hear – I don't notice it now. Beads going about their business. Under us there's the Middles, then the Lower Middles, and then... the Deeps."

"The Deeps," the young bead repeated, just to hear it said again. It sounded sinister. He imagined the layers of living beads spending lives hoping, waiting in the dark, thronging beneath where he now sat. It was a sobering thought.

"How can they *bear* it?" he whispered.

"Hey, hey, don't be so dramatic!" Pebble exclaimed. "Thousands of beads are really happy here. They're warm and dry, and think of all the friends they can make – far more than they'd ever meet on a necklace. And they can hear fully – they can't always when they're threaded. And..."

He stopped because the little bead was sobbing, the small sphere of his body shaking, his eyes overflowing with hopeless tears. Pebble looked at him.

"But I suppose it doesn't seem like that to you, does it?" he said gently.

The little bead juddered and sobbed.

"Shall I tell you about something I once saw Outside, when I was on my necklace?" asked Pebble quietly.

The sobs shuddered to a halt.

"It was a long time ago," Pebble began. "My owner put us on to go out. We travelled a long way that day – it was warm on her neck."

The little bead stared from his small tear-stained face.

"It was summer," Pebble went on. "It was still and sunlit. We went to a wheat field. It looked... It looked like gold. Hot and still and shimmering.

"And then we went right through it. We went through the wheat. It reached up to me. The tops of the stems nodded and were heavy and ripe. And then my owner –"

The small bead was holding his breath. His lips were parted.

"– and then my owner pulled some of the wheat off with her hand. And it fell into rounded, brown grains in her palm. And she said to the man she was with, 'What lovely big ears they have!'

"And they did. Large, round, brown ears."

The little bead felt a sudden shock in his wood. He, too, had large, round ears – brown like the wheat...

"That's how I knew you'd had nightmares," said Pebble.

"How –?" The little bead did not understand.

"I stayed beside you all night," said Pebble. "I wanted to because – you reminded me of the wheat ears."

The little bead was silent. He was beginning to

realise the honour of what Pebble had done. He felt suddenly humble.

"I would like your name to be Wheatear," Pebble said gently, and he turned and left.

CHAPTER 2:

BEDTIME STORIES

Wheatear had slept alone that night. Pebble had not come back, and the little bead had neither dared nor thought it prudent to seek him out. The thought of Pebble thinking he was a nuisance was so unbearable that any idea of following him was quickly dismissed.

His sleep had been better. Simply to know that there was at least one friendly bead in this desolate new environment made him a little happier. Before his eyes had fully closed he had dwelt gratefully on the best parts of Pebble's conversation.

Shortly before he awoke, he had a vision of a crowd of beads, some holding up a huge banner on which bold words were written. For some reason, inexplicable in real life but very important in his dream, Wheatear was placed at the head of the crowd and commanded to read the words to all assembled. Drawing himself up, he shouted them loudly and clearly:

"Hong Kong!"

He awoke in confusion, and cringed about him quickly. Had he really shouted? Had anyone heard? Wide-eyed with horror, he stared around his new living quarters.

It appeared that either no-one had, or no-one cared. He let out a faltering breath, his wood grain relaxing a little.

He supposed that it was morning. He sensed the general bustling activity again, and the light did seem to him to be very slightly paler that it had been before he slept. Could it be that he was getting used to the darkness? Pebble had said he would. It was The Crack that any light was coming from, the little bead knew. "Any light that is in here is the same as the light Outside," he murmured to himself. It was a comforting thought.

Except that it was so dark that it could hardly be called light – it was more a hint of slightly less blackness in the black.

Then he remembered that he had a name.

"Wheatear. Wheat–ear," he whispered, almost inaudibly, trying out the shape and sound of the word.

The bead Wheatear felt an eagerness he had not felt the day before. It was not an all-encompassing one which might be noticed by anyone else. But there was the tiniest tinge of a glow through his grain, which he alone understood.

He was feeling interest. He wanted to Know.

But he could not Know without being informed, he reasoned to himself, fully awake now. And this brought to mind his immediate problem of who to ask. It was not in his nature to strike up a conversation with a strange bead; the very thought of it made his grain begin to contract. If he was going to find out anything, it would have to be from someone he had met – but that meant scornful Amber or sniffing Mellow or that large red London bead Rough Diamond...

Of course he would have preferred Pebble to any of the others, but he had no idea when Pebble would return.

But if he was not to be alone all day, he had to find someone. Any visions his dreams had held of boldly plunging through the Bead Box had disappeared with the night. He knew that, inside, he was still the same quailing little dot of wood that he had been when he first arrived. In a sudden panic his lip began to quiver and his eyes filled.

A sudden scrunching brought him whirling round swiftly.

Discernible before him was a well-remembered outline; a worn, angular shape – the Cockney bead,

Rough Diamond. More faintly behind his bulk loomed other shapes; Wheatear recognised Amber and Mellow among them. His lips parted but no sound came out.

"And a very good mornin' to you too, Pudden," Rough Diamond said heartily. "Just come to see how you're doin'. I *surmised*," he said, as if relishing the word and rather proud of it, "as you might be in need of a bit of company."

Summoning up all his courage, the little bead remembered his manners.

"Thank you," he said. "I was just wondering whether to try and find you. And my name is Wheatear."

Rough Diamond drew himself up and opened his eyes very wide. He stared at the little brown bead before him, and then turned to the assembled company.

"His name is Wheatear," he announced with mock solemnity. "He don't like me callin' 'im Pudden, it seems. An' I can't say as I blame 'im," he added more gently under his breath.

The little bead stood with dignity.

Rough Diamond spoke again. "You were sayin'

you was thinkin' of findin' me just now. Why might that be, young *Wheatear*?" He enunciated the name carefully.

"Oh, it wasn't you especially," the little bead began to explain – but then, for fear that Rough might be hurt by this, or perhaps take offence, he went on hastily, "though of course I'm very pleased to see you –"

A sardonic sniff was heard from Mellow.

"It's just thathat," Wheatear babbled incoherently, "I was whawanting to Know things – about the Bead Box, I mean."

He raised his eyes. Amber was fixing him with a hypnotising stare.

"There's beads all around you," Amber said reasonably. "Above," – he stared upwards – "below," – he ground his 'derrière' hard on the bobbled surface, while squeaks of annoyance came from beneath him – "aaaall around," – he circled widely and returned to his former position. "Didn't you ask any of them?"

Wheatear felt broken and foolish. "No," he said lamely.

"Perhaps he was too scared," Mellow sneered, edging herself forward.

Wheatear felt smaller. This was what he had dreaded. He was surrounded by big beads, and they were all going to scorn him.

But Rough's reply took him by surprise.

"Give the little blighter a chance," he said with a hard edge to his tone. "Did you approach total strangers after your first coupla nights in this place?"

Mellow said nothing, but slunk back into the darkness.

Rough turned to look at Wheatear again. "You're pretty young to end up in 'ere," he said. "What is it you'd like to know? You've come to the right geezer – I've been 'ere long enough to tell you most things." He chuckled ruefully.

A sudden urgency lent boldness to Wheatear's words.

"But I might not 'end up' here," he said. "I might be Chosen. The Hand might Choose me. I'm an Upper Middle, and that's quite good."

Mellow sidled forward again. "Quite a little scholar," she said nastily. "Why bother to tell him anything, Rough? He seems to know it all already."

Rough ignored Mellow, but asked, "Who told you all that, young 'un?"

Before Wheatear had a chance to reply, Amber moved forward, and the small bead noticed with mingled horror and fascination how he shuffled awkwardly, never lifting either one side or the other very high. Wheatear tried to drag his eyes up to Amber's face, but they kept drifting to the lower portion of his rotund anatomy.

"No need to ask. No need to tell us," Amber began, rolling up until Wheatear's eyes were staring through his translucent stomach. "It's Pebble he's been talking to. Never keeps his pretty blue mouth shut. Dear, kind Pebble – everybody's friend," he wheedled sarcastically.

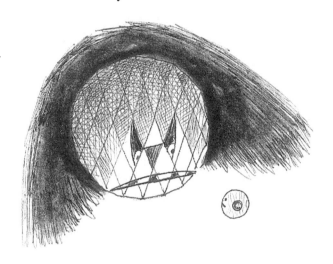

Something turned hot inside Wheatear. His burnished cheeks took on a sudden glow, and he opened his mouth to answer.

But Rough beat him to it.

"Cut it aht," he said, loudly and rather wearily. "This Wheatear's got as much right as you 'ave to be friends with who 'e likes. It sounds as if Pebble's given 'im more of a welcome than you lot 'ave.

"I've got better things to do than listen to your moanin'. I'm orf. I'll leave you to tell 'im what 'e wants to know, pore little shaver. And mind," – he directed his gaze into Amber's unconcerned eyes – "any monkey business an' you'll 'ave Rough Diamond on yer tail. Oright, sunshine?"

He nodded his scarred head at the little bead and made off into the distance.

There was a silence. The stranded beads waited in the half-light.

Then, slowly, the circle of beads around Wheatear advanced.

There was a menacing scrunching sound as bodies of plastic, glass, and ceramic moved towards him. When they were surrounding him with no spaces in between them, they stopped.

Then Amber gave a nod at Mellow, and Mellow spoke.

"Well, Pudden?" she said with deliberation. "What is it you want to know?"

What Wheatear wanted to know most at that moment was how to escape and, next, why everyone was being so nasty to him. But he had always believed that, no matter how difficult a situation was, it was always possible to go on being polite, and he resolved to do this as long as it was in his power. He did not want to open all his fears to these beads. He would save his questions for Pebble later.

Instead, he said politely, "Nothing very much in particular, thank you, Mellow. But if there's anything you'd like to tell me about life in the Bead Box, I'd be very interested to hear it."

The clearness of the bead's words and the use of her name seemed to take Mellow aback somewhat, but she said:

"All right, but you'd better listen. Shouldn't be too challenging; your ears are big enough." She turned to the other beads and smirked at the success of her joke as they nudged one another and chortled.

There was a silence again. Each looked to the other to start off. Then Mellow stared into Amber's eyes meaningfully as if communicating some message, and said:

"We'd better warn him what *can* happen in here if he's not careful."

Amber blew gently through pursed lips and shook his head as if contemplating some grave problem before he spoke.

"Terrible. Terrible. Best not to mention it — he's only young yet."

Mellow nodded.

There was silence yet again.

The little bead could not contain himself.

"Wha–what? Please tell me what can happen," he blurted.

Mellow and Amber once more exchanged glances.

"Well – I don't know…" Amber began – but as Wheatear begged again, he sighed and said, "Well – if he really wants to hear…"

"I do, I do," Wheatear said seriously.

"Very well," Amber said, as if reluctantly. He took a deep breath as if to prepare for some painful story, and at this signal the beads all crowded closer.

In the hot, tense atmosphere, Amber began.

"You're a very young bead," he reiterated, leaning forward, "and no doubt you think you know a fair bit already about the way beads lead their lives. But you know very little. V-e-r-y little," he repeated breathily, the sinister light adding glints of murky yellow to his semi-transparent body.

"You say Pebble told you that one day you might end up being Chosen by the Hand. But what he didn't tell you is that there are other ways you might End Up."

The last two words were separated and emphasised, Amber leaning nearer still.

"Pebble, it seems, also informed you that you are lucky enough to be an Upper Middle. But does it occur to you that you may not always be an Upper Middle?"

The last two words were delivered in the same manner as before, and in the hot silence Amber's speech stuck to Wheatear's mind like toffee to a tin.

"We had a bead here once," he went on, staring upwards and shaking his head regretfully, "who was an Upper Middle when he came here. He was as nice a fellow as you could wish to meet in a place like this. A long, thin bead he was. Slippery. Made of some sort of polished, shiny stuff. Lupin, his name was. V-e-r-y slippery."

Amber's eyes took on a burning quality as he fixed Wheatear with an intense gaze.

"He slipped," Amber hissed, "down, down into the Deeps. Couldn't hold himself up, see? Like quicksand. Good mate of mine, Lupin was."

Wheatear's mouth felt like a shrivelled leaf, but he found what remained of his voice.

"You mean – he's there still?"

"He's there still." Amber's gimlet eyes had never moved. "Down into the Deeps," he repeated hypnotically.

Something in the back of Wheatear's horrified wooden head tried to reason. If he were Pebble, he wouldn't be frightened. Pebble would give a sensible answer.

He was not Pebble, but he could try to be like him.

He cleared his throat with a high squeak. "But we're not like that – none of us. Long and thin, I mean – it couldn't happen to any of us. Me, for instance – could it?" he said, with an attempt at a light laugh.

"Not that particular situation, perhaps, I grant you." Amber glanced at Mellow. "But there are other things," he said ominously.

"Things – that happen in here?" Wheatear whispered.

"Not even necessarily in here," Amber said, drawing himself up. "Even when you get out of here – *if* you do – there are other things that can happen – oh, to any small, round, unsuspecting bead that happens to be out on his own..."

A small indefinable noise escaped Wheatear's lips.

"...or even *not* on his own," Amber went on in a matter-of-fact, resigned voice. "I suppose you've never *been* on your own, though, have you?"

The little bead found his voice. "Indeed I have," he squeaked indignantly. "I was alone for..."

He thought, and then decided to exaggerate a little.

"...weeks and weeks when my necklace broke, lying on the cold floor. Quite alone."

"In that case," Amber said heavily, "you were lucky to escape The Lung."

Wheatear's wood seemed to become stone as he waited for fresh horrors to be disclosed to him. Mellow pushed forward. Her green eyes narrowed. 'Mellow' meant 'softened', Wheatear knew – like a melon at its finest. But if this bead was a melon, she would be under-ripe, hard and bitter. There was nothing honeydew about Mellow.

"Where did you fall, when you were 'quite alone'?" she asked, her voice edged with sarcasm.

"I was behind a cabinet," replied Wheatear, wondering what had prompted Mellow's question.

Mellow and Amber nodded knowingly.

"That would explain it," Mellow said, receding again.

Amber lurched towards the small bead and thrust his glistening features into Wheatear's face. He breathed his words hoarsely.

"The Lung Sucks," he enunciated murderously. "The Hand works it. It crawls along the floor, searching for the vile detritus of human life, among which may lie" – he allowed his gaze to drift over Wheatear's features – "young beads such as yourself.

"We are told," Amber went on portentously, "that, once The Lung is poised to Suck, there is no known method of escape. The victim, it would seem, dies through suffocation in the stinking morass of foulness which is part of humanity's existence – and upon which The Lung thrives."

Silence heated the air.

"Tell him how it roars," Mellow put in with horrible eagerness.

"No!" Wheatear squeaked involuntarily. "I mean, no thank you. I can quite see how lucky I was to be behind the cabinet. I was probably as safe there as on my necklace." His controlled voice belied his true emotions, which were those of the very essence of horror.

"Would that it were true," sighed Amber, looking upwards again, and then casting his eyes down as if in deep regret. "Unfortunately, even *there* you're far from safe. But there it is – I've talked enough." He began to stretch as if putting an end to the conversation.

"Wait!" Wheatear cried, grasped by a kind of desperate need to hear further appalling revelations while he could. "I can't believe you're not safe on a necklace. Tell me what can happen there."

"*Has* happened," Amber said gloomily. "A most small, round, shiny little bead" – he eyed Wheatear's polished circular surface – "was once Chosen out of here to be strung up. An Upper Middle, I seem to recall – made a nice centrepiece. Necklace was given to a little girl. A sad end. Pity – he was a grand little chap." He blinked away an apparent misting in his eyes.

"But – what happened?" Wheatear demanded.

Mellow came closer. "Drowned," she said, her yellow teeth showing as her lips pulled back to frame the single word.

Wheatear stared.

"She sucked her necklace," Amber whispered sibilantly. "Sleep tight, Pudden."

And, gathering his cronies around him, Amber shuffled off with his characteristic movement, the sound of their laughter diminishing like the point of a sword.

CHAPTER 3:
I WILL ALWAYS KNOW WHERE HE IS

How long Wheatear cried that night, he never knew – but he did know that, when he woke, the wood around his eyes felt raw and unpolished.

The first things those eyes saw were the two concerned faces of Pebble and Rough Diamond staring down at him.

"'E's come to," Rough breathed huskily.

Wheatear wondered who he meant – and then with a slight shock understood that Rough was referring to him. He became wider awake. Pebble had not replied, but Wheatear heard a long exhaled breath from his direction which sounded to be one of relief. He stared back at the two onlookers.

The second he took in their faces, he realised that he had caused them great worry. They must have been preparing for their own sleep when they came across him – young, foolish, incapable, blubbering... It was the second time Pebble had put up with his tears. What must they think of him? What a picture he must present – weak, whimpering... It was pathetic. He had to apologise.

"I'm sorry," he said – but a splintery noise came out, as if his very wood's soul had been wrung of its moisture.

But they had heard him. Both spoke at once, in a torrent of reassurance.

"Sorry? No!" "Not you that should be sorry!"

Their voices – one clear and mature, one deeper with a slight grate – were a blessing to him. Like a creature deprived of water, he waited to drink in more.

"We're the ones who should be sorry – truly," Pebble said seriously, with a slightly embarrassed dropping of the eyes.

Wheatear was impressed by Pebble's use of the word 'truly', and thought it added great weight to his sentence. He decided to use it in the future.

"Aren't we, Rough?" Pebble continued, glancing at the rugged red bead.

"Yeah," Rough said, looking equally discomfited. "Aw, little 'un – I don't know what to say. I ought never to 'ave gorn orf an' left you with that lot, but – well, I 'ad important things to see to, know what I mean?"

Wheatear didn't, but supposed that Rough must be very busy.

"When I came back 'ere with Pebble an' saw you doused out with tears, an' yer pore eyes swollen shut an' so sore you could have struck a match on 'em... Blimey, it were terrible. I'll never forgive meself."

Wheatear had not seen it this way – and while touched by Rough's speech and most moved by the account of his own appearance, he was horrified to think that Rough might take all the blame upon himself.

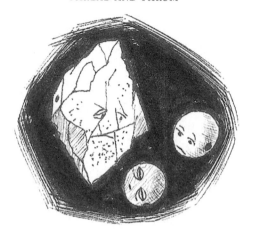

"Oh, no, really, R– er, Mr. Diamond," he jabbered respectfully, "please, please don't blame yourself. It was my fault for staying and listening to them..."

He stopped. How did Rough and Pebble know what he had been listening to?

Pebble read his thoughts. "Yes, you heard a lot, didn't you?" he said. "The good old horror stories, eh?"

Wheatear hung his head. He couldn't remember anything good about them.

"They'll not try it again," Rough stated frankly. "That's for sure."

"W–won't they?" Wheatear piped up, hope darting into him.

Pebble cleared his throat uneasily, and glanced at Rough. A grim expression had spread over the latter's weathered features, and a pragmatic look had come into his eyes. He drew himself up and flashed a look down at himself, then at Wheatear.

With a sudden spurt of mingled horror and excitement, Wheatear saw that a fresh cleft adorned Rough's time-scarred exterior.

"You haven't – *fought* them?" he asked in alarm. No matter how unpleasant or fearsome the characters concerned, Wheatear felt sure that fighting was wrong.

Rough's grim look spread still further. "Didn't have much choice," he responded heavily. "Jumped on me when I was asleep."

Wheatear was shocked. He tried to imagine what it must be like to be deeply asleep, and to be woken by the full weight of two malicious and fairly large beads landing on his body.

"They didn't like Rough standing up for you," Pebble explained, "and that was their way of showing it. There were several witnesses. A dreadful way to wake up –"

"You're tellin' me," Rough put in with an unamused half-laugh. "Worst alarm clock I've ever 'ad."

"– but they hadn't reckoned on Rough's quick thinking and strength," Pebble continued, "nor how popular he is. Quite a few beads came to his assistance, and delivered a few body punches I'm afraid. Amber and Mellow soon backed off."

Wheatear did not know what to think. He was certain that he ought not to feel pleased that Amber and Mellow had been attacked, but all the time he was aware that he rather liked the idea. He did quail a little on wondering how the other beads back home – the ones he had been threaded with on his necklace – would react if they could see him now. He was sure they would disapprove. They had been such very well-behaved little beads, and so had he. Yet here he was, chatting to this large, red-faced Londoner, who got jumped on and involved in fights – for his sake.

A meek tingling passed through Wheatear's wood at the thought of this. Rough had gone through this for *him*. He wondered if that meant Rough might like him a little bit. He liked Rough, he thought – though he was rather cruel-looking and frightening. But perhaps he couldn't help how he looked.

All these thoughts passed through Wheatear as

Rough stood before him. Wheatear looked again, fascinated, at the newly-hewn gash on Rough's broad front. Rough was so much bigger than Wheatear's small brown self.

"Are you hurt?" he enquired politely.

"Nah – just a scratch," Rough replied gruffly, although it didn't look like a scratch to Wheatear.

"How about you?" Pebble asked quietly. "Are you all right? You've not had an easy start, have you?"

The little blob of wood sat before him.

"You know, you mustn't listen to a lot of what they say," Pebble continued, the vague light from the Crack illuminating one side of his smooth blue-grey body.

"Why? Isn't it true?" Wheatear asked, hoping very hard in his wood that it might not be.

Pebble paused and drew a breath. "It *is* true," he began – but, as Wheatear's woodknots sank, he explained, "There are lots of things that are true and terrible in the world. It's just that we can't spend all our time thinking and worrying about them. I mean, you were happy Outside, weren't you? You liked being on your necklace?"

Wheatear's expression became rapt. "Oh yes," he breathed, "I loved my necklace."

"And I dare say you'd like to go back, wouldn't you? I mean, you'd go back if you had the chance?"

"Oh yes," Wheatear said again. "I should – so love it." He tried not to feel that sad feeling again, but his wood ached inside.

"And if you were back on your necklace, would you spend all day in terror, wondering whether your owner was going to drown you?" Pebble's eyes stared candidly into his.

The little bead pondered. He had not thought of it like that before. Pebble was very clever, he decided.

"No," he said. "I should just be happy, and enjoy being in peace again."

Pebble's eyes smiled at him. "Do the same here," he said.

Wheatear's large eyes looked up at him. "I will," he said solemnly. He felt as if he was making a vow.

But as suddenly as his fear left him, it bounded back, and the spell of his vow was broken. He had lost his nerve.

"Oh but Pebble, I can't! I can't do it!" he wailed in panic. "It sounds so easy, but I never know where you are, and there's this noise of strangers all the time, and you're both so brave and I'm so small and plain, and..."

The words came tumbling out.

Pebble shut his eyes and smiled in a patient way before briefly regarding Rough. "You couldn't get much plainer than us two," he said in a matter-of-fact voice.

Wheatear considered the pair before him. He supposed that Rough was plain, but not in the way he himself was. Rough's name was plain too. But as for Pebble, Wheatear did not think he was plain at all. He thought his blue, lake-smooth surface was beautiful, and he liked his name very much.

So he didn't answer, because he couldn't say that one was plain and not the other.

Pebble, as usual, seemed to read his thoughts. "I chose my name myself," he said. "It was another thing that happened Outside."

Pebble looked a little awkward, as if he wasn't sure that others would want to be bored by his tales. But Wheatear was agog. He loved to hear about the Outside. He longed to hear how Pebble chose his name, and said so.

Pebble began: "My owner –"

"The one that went into the wheat field?" Wheatear interrupted breathlessly.

"The lady, yes, that went into the wheat field," Pebble said. "She loved being outside. Outside her house, I mean," he explained, seeing Wheatear's confused expression. "She once wore us when she went to the sea."

"The sea!" the little bead said wistfully. He had never seen the sea, though he had heard of it.

"Yes; she walked on the beach, with us round her neck," Pebble went on. "I looked down and saw her bare feet treading and sinking. She was walking on thousands and thousands of smooth, sea-washed pebbles – thousands of them, Wheatear! And all outside. That was the surface of the beach."

A strange intensity had come into Pebble's voice, and his eyes seemed focused on something distant.

"She would lift handfuls of them up, so that I saw them quite clearly. I watched them, sifting through her fingers. They were the colours of the sea, the sky, and the rain. The sea had washed them smooth and dull. They reminded me of – myself."

His eyes jerked back to Wheatear, but he did not

smile. His voice became more muted.

"Then she walked into the sea," he murmured, "and I looked at her feet in the water. They trod on pebbles. More and more pebbles, blue and smoothed, washed, washed by the endless movement. They seemed at peace," he finished simply.

"She must have been very happy," Wheatear whispered, his face alight.

"She was crying," Pebble said, and looked at nothing.

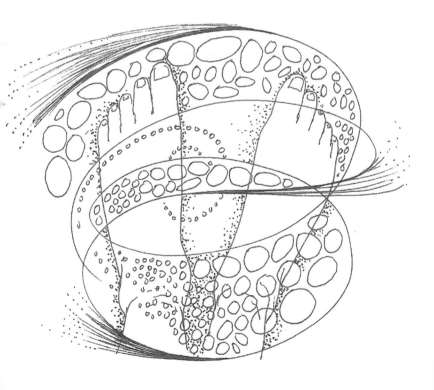

There was a silence now in the Bead Box, where innumerable beads waited in darkness. Rough's even breathing formed a rhythm in the quiet, like the tide over shingle. Wheatear felt older and wiser, he realised. There were good things, and bad things. In – and out. In – and out. The breathing went on. Good things and bad things. Endlessly washing, In things and Out things... His eyelids began to droop.

"You're tired," Pebble said gently. "Are your eyes still sore?"

Wheatear looked up at him. "A bit," he said. "They'll get better now."

"No more tears, eh?" Rough grunted, awkwardly but kindly. He was like a huge, burly boxer with a tiny, delicate baby. He did not know how to talk to this small, vulnerable creature.

Wheatear saw his discomfort and was filled with a sudden warmth towards him. "I'll try," he promised. "I suppose it's just – hard at first." He smiled bravely.

"It is," Pebble said, offering the truth, as always, rather than well-meaning pretence. "But you've got all the potential to manage very well. That's why I'm not going to let myself worry about what you said."

"What did I say?" Wheatear asked, more awake now.

"You said you never know where I am," Pebble said, "and that's how it should be, Wheatear. It's no good knowing where I am, or Rough, or anyone else is, all the time. You've got to learn things for yourself. I'm not going to stay with you."

"Aw, Peb, 'ave some pity on the pore little beggar!" Rough interjected with a look of anguish. "Look what 'appened when I wen' orf an' left 'im!"

But Pebble turned on him. "No, Rough," he said firmly. "We both know what I have to do. Wheatear could stay with me all day if he liked, and learn practically nothing. Or he could spend much of his time discovering this way of life for himself. These last two days he has learned a lot –"

"Yeah – but look at it!" Rough burst out. "What an experience. It's all bin bad – nuffin' but bad!"

"I agree," said Pebble reasonably. "Until now, it has. I remember my first few days were not much better. But there are good things and bad things –"

Wheatear gave a little start. "Yes," he said, in a strange voice.

"– and you've hit on the very word for it,

Rough," Pebble continued. "'Experience'. Without experiencing life in the Bead Box in his own way, Wheatear would be a very dull bead indeed. But he's not going to be dull."

He turned back to Wheatear.

"You know, don't you, that I'd be more than happy to have you with me all day?"

A warm glow passed through Wheatear. He did not reply.

"But that really would be no good," Pebble said. "No good at all. You do see that, don't you? You do understand?"

Again Wheatear made no reply. He knew that inside he did not understand, he did not see. He wanted to be with Pebble, or even Rough, all day long; he would like it. He did not see why it was so impossible.

But in the same moment he realised that, on every occasion that he had spoken to Pebble so far, Pebble's advice had been right – so he decided it was best to go on following it.

Pebble seemed to take Wheatear's silence as disagreement. "It's hard for you, I know," he said, "but I want you to grow up by learning how you can deal with things that happen to you, not how I can deal with them for you. We'll see each other lots –"

"But never lettin' the pore little blighter know where you are, Peb!" Rough said pleadingly. "'Ave an' 'eart! Don't you reckon that's a bit 'arsh?"

"Not at all," Pebble said quietly. "You see, I will always know where *he* is. I promise."

The dim grey light gloomed the blue of Pebble's smooth domed back as, with a last look at the large and small figures before him, he made his way deeper into the blackness and was lost to sight.

The silence when he had disappeared seemed impenetrable – yet Wheatear could still sense a distant vibration, beads' lives being lived in the layers.

Perhaps he was getting used to it.

Rough finally cleared his throat and stared down at the tiny, docile being towards whom he now felt so protective.

"Well, so long, little un," he said gruffly, with the same awkwardness he had shown before. "Things to do. You do as yer bin told, yeah? Like me an' Pebble do. Best way."

Wheatear knew it should have been "like Pebble and I do," but he did not say so. "Goodbye, Rough," he said clearly. "Thank you so much."

Rough coughed again. "Well, I'll be orf, then," he said. The half-light caught the deep scar on his broad chest as he turned quickly to go.

Before he had travelled very far he wheeled round again.

"Anyway," he said in a loud whisper, "Rough'll be there for you, mate, when you need 'im. You remember." He set his lips in a decisive line and scrunched into the distance.

Once again Wheatear was alone. But what a different sort of aloneness to the other times, he thought! He let the stillness sink into him. There was so much to growing up. So much to think about. He had to do what Pebble said, and not follow him around always. Pebble had given Wheatear that advice for his own good.

Then Wheatear remembered that Pebble had said he would be happy – no, *more* than happy – to have him there all day if it would have helped. The warm glow returned to the wood of Wheatear. He repeated the phrase under his breath.

"More than happy." He tried stressing the syllables in various ways.

As he did so, his still-swollen lids once more found themselves drooping, despite the weak, silvery light from the far-off, unknown Crack which told thousands of beads whether it was day or night. The learning brain of Wheatear drifted with numerous impressions. Sea-washed stones, rain-blue, grey as tears, and seaweed green, tumbled in slow motion ever downwards. Pebble would always know where he was. Hands worn and smooth plunged into water dry as shingle, and brought it up brittle as beads – lovingly, tenderly. Gentle fingers singled him out, selected his shape, would surely Choose him.

Yes, please Choose me, prayed the half-dreaming Wheatear as he dwelt on the day's events.

Pebble was right about good things and bad things, but the little brown bead who slept in the shadowy layers of the Bead Box would still rather have been Outside than In.

CHAPTER 4:
BEING WILLED

Some hours later, Wheatear gradually awoke. His breathing was even and he felt rested. When he had come fully to his senses, he saw that the pearly half-light in which he had fallen asleep had dwindled to a smooth, inky blue – not yet at its blackest – which told him that it was evening. The wearing background noise was quieter.

He felt comfortable, and his mind was, for the moment, in a state of calmness. This was such an unusual feeling after the turmoil of the previous days that Wheatear questioned why it should be. Slowly he began to remember what had happened before he slept.

He had enjoyed that lovely talk with Pebble and Rough. A sudden sharp appreciation of their friendship warmed him. What differences there were between beads! He compared his two friends with Amber and Mellow, and found it very worrying. He was still very frightened. He knew he would have to meet those beads again.

Rough had said he would be there for him when he needed him – but how could he be? And how could Wheatear find him, when Rough had "important things to do?"

As more memories came back to him, he was able to think more clearly than in his soporific state a few hours earlier. There was so much to work at, it seemed to the little bead. He was very young to be all alone – but there was in his wood an innocent eagerness, a will to strive to do anything which would help him learn to be a better bead. Now as he sat – a small shining sphere lost among a mass of others tougher, older and more confident than himself – he thought of what he should do to make more good things than bad things happen in his life.

"It's quite right; Pebble spoke the truth," the little bead reasoned. "I must find things out for myself.

It's true that I'm very much alone," – here he gulped – "but Pebble promised that he would always know where I am. He *promised*."

"Promise" seemed a very solemn word to Wheatear. He knew that it was wrong to break a promise, and he was sure that Pebble would never break one. That must mean that Pebble knew where he was right now. Rather self-consciously he looked behind him. Pebble was not there. He turned, looking carefully in a full circle. Neither Pebble nor Rough was anywhere to be seen. And yet he was sure he was being watched. He felt as if Pebble was there, guiding him and taking care of him, willing him to do something.

Yes – that was it. He was being willed to do something. As soon as it came into his mind, Wheatear knew that was the feeling he had been trying to pin down.

But what was it that he was supposed to do?

His thoughts were cut short by a faint but unmistakable sound somewhere ahead of him. A pleasant anticipation filled his wood. Could it be Rough and Pebble coming to see if he had slept well? Wheatear began to speculate upon the new questions he could now ask them.

But it is not always wise to speculate. As the noise grew more distinct, it became apparent that neither Rough nor Pebble was causing it. For the sound was that of a soft, uneven shuffling, accompanied by an occasional disgruntled sniff or a whine of complaint.

Amber and Mellow were approaching.

Instinctively, Wheatear's wood grain pulled itself in tight at the knowledge of their presence. In the near darkness they could not be seen, nor could they see him, until they were very close. Wheatear, rooted to the spot, was undecided as to what to do.

By lurking in the shadows, it was possible that they would miss him altogether. But on the other hand they might see that he was deliberately attempting to hide from them, and would laugh, loudly and scornfully, at his terror. The thought of this was unendurable. Wheatear knew that it was no good hiding from trouble. That was one of the things that Pebble had tried to help him understand. He *did* understand – or rather, he had at the time – but somehow now it didn't seem quite so easy.

Meanwhile, the shuffling grew louder, and seemed less rhythmic than usual. Wheatear found the noise both sinister and irritating. To adopt such an inconvenient way of moving around simply to obscure a ridiculous secret which everyone knew anyway seemed ludicrous. Compared with Pebble's honest, open approach to life, Amber's attitude seemed self-centred and childish.

But Wheatear's first impression had been correct. He had discerned a slight new unsteadiness in Amber's grinding gait – and, as Amber and Mellow drew near enough for Wheatear to see them, he saw that Amber made difficult, uneven movements and appeared to be short of breath. Mellow seemed even more bitter than usual. Any second now, they would see him.

Summoning all his failing courage, Wheatear remained standing in their path. He lifted his face and looked bravely at them, his heart thudding like a wooden pendulum wound to the wrong speed.

The two older beads faced him.

With something beating high in his throat, Wheatear said:

"Hello."

The stertorous breathing stopped. The shuffling ceased. Mellow was half shielded by Amber's thick figure, and Wheatear could see portions of her livid lemon colour through the translucent dull gold of the nearer bead.

The two beads stared unblinkingly at Wheatear. Not a sound broke the silence. It was as if the whole Bead Box waited.

Slowly, Wheatear's eyes were forced away from their sphinx-like gaze. Slowly, they travelled downwards over the bodies of the newcomers – and what they saw made them freeze into immobility.

Marring the shining surface of Amber's glossy front was a huge graze, extending right across his stomach and disappearing round the side of his body. The force of it had been enough to remove all the shine from the area, so that it had become opaque, looking as if it had been grated.

Mellow, waiting just behind him, also arrested Wheatear's gaze. One of her green stripes seemed slightly different from the others. As Wheatear looked more deliberately he saw that, following the line of the stripe and almost camouflaged by it, there was a deep crack penetrating into Mellow's interior, like a fine knife wound. Wheatear could only imagine what force of blow it would have taken to crack open the surface of a bead's body.

Wheatear's expression was one of horror. He could make no sound.

After an unmeasured length of acute silence – which was in reality a few seconds – the two beads, maimed and weary, moved past Wheatear without words or further look, and were lost in darkness.

Wheatear remained rooted to the spot, still staring at the space where they had stood. His body seemed to be a frozen block, incapable of feeling. Eventually he turned and slowly lowered himself face down into the Bead Box, his eyes remaining open. There he lay, staring downwards, his thoughts halted by the vile vision he had just seen.

There were good things and bad things – but surely violence could not be right. He was very serious now. The knowledge that his arrival had occasioned these things was only too clear to him. Had he not come, two beads might never have suffered the violence that had possibly damaged their powers of movement and certainly their looks.

Overcome by this responsibility, Wheatear gave a groan and pushed his body deeper down as if trying to cover himself from sight. He knew that he could not go on in this way. He had to do something – change something.

As he stared into the black, the memory of what he had been puzzling over before the arrival of the wounded beads came insistently back to him. Yes: he had been trying to find out what he felt he was being willed to do. He was even surer of it now that this last incident had taken place. The feeling of being meant to do something was very strong.

As he struggled with this persistent idea, Pebble's promise about always knowing where he was kept clanging in his mind. Eventually it clanged so loudly that the poor bead could not hope to ignore it. He tried to clarify his thoughts by repeating it, still face down in the Bead Box.

"'I will always know where *he* is,'" muttered Wheatear as he puzzled in his small wooden head. He muttered it again.

His whirring brain felt so stuffed with confusion that it must have given up, for he woke with a gasp of terror a while later, still face down. For a moment his panic was intense, but he gradually realised that he was surfacing from a nightmare.

He had dreamed that Mellow, damaged of body and evil of mind, had plunged down on him from a great height, intent on ploughing him down to the Deeps as he lay with his face staring downwards. Then, at the crucial moment, Rough and Pebble had suddenly shot in on either side, intent on attacking Mellow and coming to his rescue.

This would not do, Wheatear thought soberly. He realised what his dream showed. He was relying totally on his poor friends to get him out of every danger. He could not expect them to do such things for him. He had to simply face it; he had to help himself.

A second later he sat vertically upright. He had got it: a new meaning to Pebble's words, one that he had not seen before.

Of course Pebble would always know where he was. Because he never moved!

Ever since he had arrived in the Bead Box, Wheatear had listened, despaired, slept, cried and talked in the very same place where he now stood.

Now he understood what he had to do to help himself. He had to move from that spot. Pebble must have said what he did under the assumption that Wheatear would always remain in that same place.

A feeling of shame spread through him. What a boring, helpless stick-in-the-mud Pebble must think him, to announce with such certainty that he would always know where he was! It seemed almost a hurtful remark. But Wheatear felt certain that Pebble would not say anything of that sort without a reason. Everything Pebble said was always of benefit, designed to help him. So could Pebble have meant this remark to help Wheatear in some way?

Slowly the realisation dawned on him. That was it. Pebble had made this comment purely to bring about that slight shame in Wheatear – to pique him into action. A smile of amazed admiration flickered on Wheatear's mouth as he saw that he had fallen absolutely into the gentle trap Pebble had set for him. What Pebble had said had been nothing less than a little hint to get moving – soft enough for him to miss it at first, but just sharp enough to make him take it up. Pebble was helping him to help himself.

He stood motionless, extremely impressed by the cleverness of the blue bead who had managed to create such an influence on him in such a short time. He reflected on what Pebble had done with his own time in the Bead Box. He seemed so mature and knowledgeable. How had he managed it?

Wheatear guessed that it had taken a lot of hard work for Pebble to get where he was. Pebble was a grown-up, Wheatear was sure. He seemed to be able to tell genuine beads from false ones. Wheatear could only blunder on, learning by mere chance who would treat him well and who would not. It just seemed a matter of luck, he thought bitterly.

But perhaps it was not. How carefully Pebble observed – both Inside and Outside. Would Wheatear ever have noticed the stamp when Amber bent over? Pebble had. And look at the detailed memories Pebble still carried of his life Outside. The colours, atmosphere, and surroundings were all brought to life when Pebble described them. It occurred to Wheatear that Pebble must look very hard at things.

But it was not just things like that. Wheatear had often noticed how intently Pebble listened when another bead spoke. He always waited to hear what they had to say before giving his own opinion. Perhaps Wheatear could listen more closely to the words of others.

He sifted through the conversation he had last had. He recalled Pebble saying to Rough, "We both know what I have to do."

"Well, I wish *I* did," Wheatear muttered.

Rough would probably have said, "Me an' you both know," – and Wheatear smiled, slightly surprised to find that the thought of Rough gave him a warm feeling. With pleasure he remembered the gruff voice saying, "You do as yer bin told, like me an' Pebble." It wasn't his place to find fault with Rough's grammar. That was just Rough's way.

His smile faded and he sat up further. What did that actually mean? What had Rough and Pebble been told to do? And by whom?

Then he remembered that Pebble had made the journey to the Crack by himself, just to satisfy his own curiosity. Fancy pushing your way, upwards, through the protesting bodies of thousands of others struggling for survival, just to catch a glimpse of the Outside for yourself! The very thought of the terrifying journey, the rigorous climb, all alone, not knowing if or when you would return to your own layer, made Wheatear's wood quake. He was sure he couldn't do it.

In despair he still stood in the now impenetrable blackness of the Box. He had to do *something*. If he didn't try, he would never be able to face himself again, let alone Pebble. Rough would probably take pity on him, but he did not want pity. He must not continue to be this helpless, blubbering little blob. He must show himself that he could do it.

But do what? The poor insignificant morsel of wood almost rolled to and fro in anguish. He knew he did not dare push his way through all those beads to the Crack. He knew nothing of the Highs, nor indeed of any other beads, and he was frightened of them.

Then could he go sideways? He thought of what lay sideways. He supposed that somewhere was the side of the Box. He could go to that. Yes; he would go along his own layer, touch the side of the Box, and then come back again. He could tell Pebble that he had been. He would have to go in a very straight line, and as soon as he reached the side he would come back again, very straight, so that he would not get lost.

Perhaps that was what he was being willed to do, told to do. And Rough had said: "You do as yer bin told, like me an' Pebble."

Should he speak to anyone on the way? Memories of his first night came dancing with dark shapes, clawing, mocking. He hid his face. He would have to meet so many more strangers.

He wailed inwardly. They might all be like Amber or Mellow!

Or they might all be like Pebble, he reasoned more sensibly. It was no good being frightened. He would do what he knew to be right, as he always tried to do. If anyone spoke to him, he would answer as politely as he could. It was always the right thing to do, to be polite whatever others were like...

Thus, after feverishly planning long into the night, Wheatear was left to gain what rest he could for the journey ahead.

He did not know that his journey was never to take place.

CHAPTER 5:
TRAUMA AND A TRICK

How lovely it is to wake slowly, to lie in the warm and to feel the comfort of your resting place around you. Wheatear was in that state between sleeping and waking – a cushioned, fleecy consciousness, knowing that something pleasant was receding and something new was approaching.

It was in this relaxed state that he first heard the grumbling.

He lay with his eyes closed, aware that a vibration was travelling through him – not just the usual thrum. Something else was different, but he was still unwilling to open his eyes.

Then, as he became definitely awake, he realised that the feeble ash-grey morning glimmer of the Bead Box was far lighter than usual – so bright that he was now *unable* to lift his eyelids.

Faintly worried, he peeped from the corner of one scrunched-up eye, listening to the increasing noise. It was a persistent churning and mumbling, and it seemed to be coming from way above him. It was soon impossible to ignore it.

Nor could he escape the light. As he stood upright, exposing his ears, the noise blasted louder, grinding like some uncomfortably close machine.

Before he had time to sort his thoughts, a vast, fork-like creature grazed past him and thrust into the bodies of thousands of screaming beads.

A high noise rang in his ears, coming from his own throat.

The warm, fleshy fork, revoltingly soft, cleaved the layers of the Bead Box, sending Wheatear and countless others tumbling into space.

Almost fainting with terror, Wheatear was hurled against the hard bodies of his fellows. The roar of cascading beads and the loud cries of fear were forced into his head. At one point he was raised to a sickening height and held in space, feeling the bodies of others trickling out of the hold and hurtling far below. As they fell and he was lifted, the brilliance of the unaccustomed light struck him like a fierce blow, threatening to split open his wood with piercing rays.

This was followed by an appalling drop which knocked the breath out of his body. As he lay choking and gasping, ill with fear and unable to think of anything but the pain of his own surface, the rumbling and churning ceased.

There was a moment's silence – then an ear-splitting crash and the return of darkness.

There was a stunned atmosphere broken only by the vague moaning of bruised and traumatised beads.

Then came several reassuring voices from various directions – the old comforting the young, the unhurt tending the injured, and the brave calming the fearful.

Wheatear lay almost fully upside down, breathing. He could focus only on this for the moment – nothing else. His eyes were closed, his wood throbbed and his body felt huge and grotesque.

Soon, the possibilities of his physical appearance

filtered through to him. He hardly dared open his eyes for fear of what he might see. Indefinable images of Amber's and Mellow's injuries flashed through his mind. Supposing he was to see such things on his own self?

He knew he'd have to open his eyes soon, but in the few seconds before he did he tried to prepare himself. It was likely that, even if he was not shocked by his own body, he would be shocked by the bodies of the beads around him.

With a sudden snap he came back to reality. Who *were* the beads around him? Where was he?

Rolling as quickly as he dared, he righted himself and opened his eyes.

Casting a wary look downwards first, he made a quick survey of his condition – which to his immense relief was far less marked than his pain seemed to suggest. After an intent examination, he was satisfied that he had escaped unscathed.

He now turned his eyes to his surroundings. It might have been his dazed state, but he was almost sure that it was darker here than in his original place. Desperately he glanced at the faces and shapes of those around him. Not one was familiar.

A weak panic that had sprung up within him gave way to a slow acceptance of his situation.

Listening to nearby conversations, he realised that at least some of these beads were clearly in similar circumstances to his own. Some were more hurt than he was, and he saw that he had been lucky. He watched as one moss-green oval bead rubbed its surface against the bruised exterior of another – probably a total stranger – to soothe it. Everywhere were examples of sympathy and help.

But the strangeness of the whole morning worried Wheatear. He, too, needed guidance and reassurance.

After looking around him, he rolled on his poor, sore little bottom to face the green bead, who was now standing back and surveying the results of her care. She did not see Wheatear waiting patiently behind her.

He gave a polite little cough. Getting no response, he leaned his body against the stranger's and gave two gentle taps.

"Eh? Oh, hello there, another newcomer. Are you in one piece?" the green bead gasped, looking worn out.

"I'm quite well, thank you," Wheatear said in his high, clear voice, "but I would very much like to know what happened just now."

"What hap–? Ah, I see, you really are a newcomer," said the green bead, looking Wheatear up and down. "Well, it's quite simple really. Have you heard of the Hand at all?"

"Oh yes," piped the little bead eagerly, to save the green bead the trouble of explaining.

Then something began to occur to him, and his features fell in disbelief.

"Tha– that wasn't the Hand, was it?" he questioned huskily. He dreaded the answer.

"Certainly was, my dear," the green bead said. "It was Choosing again. It's happened twice before in my Boxtime, but never this early in the morning."

Wheatear was silent for a moment; then "Thank you," he said, almost inaudibly. He turned, leaving the mossy oval bead to minister to others in need, and shambled away, shattered.

He found a small hollow among recuperating beads, and sat to think. He remembered only too well how the Hand had picked at him behind the cupboard, and dropped him from a height – but that Hand was tidying up. He had thought that when the Hand came Choosing, it would be so different. He smiled bitterly. He had imagined some kindly, soft-coloured creature gently probing, noticing his wood grain, tenderly picking and singling him out. But this – the blinding light, the ghastly noises of the wounded, the rooting up of young and old from their home layers...

Wheatear shut his eyes. He knew now that he had been a very foolish small bead indeed.

The deepest hurt he felt, deep inside his wood, so deep that he could never tell anyone, was that he had not been Chosen. The huge chance that he had waited for had come, and had passed, and there was no telling if or when it would come again. Tears again made small matching silver beads of his eyes, but angrily he willed them away. He would not cry. It was a waste of time.

The full realisation of just how many beads there were in the Bead Box came upon him. It was a hopeless waste of energy, this endless anticipation. He was one of thousands, all of them hoping to end up on some necklace or bracelet or embroidery. He had not even met a bead who matched him, so he could not be threaded to make a symmetrical pattern, nor even used as an eye on some stuffed toy. He would never be Chosen as a centrepiece because he was so ordinary. There were literally hundreds of others more beautiful than he, some exceptionally so.

Again, Wheatear felt suddenly older.

By the time Wheatear broke from his solitary day-dreaming, he had reached several conclusions. The first was that he needed to discover in what part of the Bead Box he now found himself. The second was that he needed to brush away the feelings of blank despair and hopelessness that threatened to swamp him, and try to make practical and sensible plans for returning to his original layer – for he was convinced that this was not the Upper Middles. It still seemed darker, and the atmosphere felt different.

But the third and most important decision was that he had, at all costs, to find Pebble. Pebble had said that he must not follow him about, and that he would always know where he was, but that had been in very different circumstances. Pebble now had no way of knowing Wheatear's whereabouts. Pebble had probably been scooped up by the Hand and deposited elsewhere in the Bead Box – or even...

But Wheatear would not allow himself to think this last thought.

The heart of his wood again weakened within him as he contemplated the immensity of his task. But he decided that he must be brave and start with one small try.

"Great oaks from little acorns grow," Wheatear said earnestly to himself. He had heard someone say it once, when he had been Outside, and it always gave him comfort.

He sighed and stretched his wood a little, and looked up.

A start went through him as he saw that he was being watched.

Directly opposite him were six bright little eyes, all identical, and all fixed on him.

They belonged to three small bodies, all as round and as red and as shiny as three miniature juicy berries.

Wheatear stared back.

"Day-dreamer! Wakey-wakey-wakey!" came a shrill voice, followed by peals of giggling from three little faces.

Wheatear couldn't help smiling. It was so long since he had heard anybody laugh.

"I'm Robin," said the first bright little bead.

"And I'm Pippin –"

"– and I'm Cherry," followed the others, beaming brightly too.

"We're together," the three added, in unison.

"So you're triplets. I'm Wheatear," said Wheatear, unable to dislike this rosy trio.

"What's a wheatear?" the first of the three enquired interestedly.

"I– it's an Ear of Wheat," said Wheatear, taken aback. He had not expected to be asked this question.

"Then it's just right," the third little triplet declared, "'cos you are mostly ear. And now we want to help you," she concluded immediately, before Wheatear could decide his exact reaction to her remark.

"You're lost, aren't you?" Pippin said, as if being lost was one of the pleasantest things that could happen to someone.

Wheatear opened his mouth to speak.

"We're just above the Lower Middles," Robin piped up, answering Wheatear's unspoken question.

Wheatear closed his mouth again.

"You don't say much, do you?" Cherry said, and again they collapsed into gigglings.

"We never let anyone say anything," Pippin said, still smiling. "We're always getting told off for it. *Now!!!*" he shrilled suddenly. "Laughter – halt! Stand-still-heads-up-tummies-in siblings…! The Ear of Wheat wishes to get a word in edgeways."

The three tiny beads pulled themselves into a line, straightened up as if fit to pop, and looked expectantly at Wheatear.

The bewildered brown bead considered the three

young matching ones before him, and took advantage of their temporary silence to put the question that puzzled him most.

"How come you're still together?"

The three little beads relaxed, and Cherry answered his question. "Pippin woke up earlier than we did," she explained. "He was having a funny dream," – here she glanced at the other two and giggled – "and he suddenly woke up. As he lay on his back," – here she put on a fearful face and ghostly voice – "he heard a gra-a-a-ating noise fa-a-a-r above him, and it seemed to be getting lighter..."

"Whoo-oo-ooh," Pippin whispered, while Robin did a ghostly dance behind them. Cherry giggled and nudged them both away.

"He immediately guessed that the lid of our Box was being opened, and Feared the Worst," Cherry went on impressively. "So being such a sensible young bead," – here Pippin knocked her for her sarcasm, and there was more giggling – "he woke us up at once and we all went straight for the side."

Wheatear frowned a little. He did not understand.

"Perhaps you don't know about that trick?" Cherry said kindly. "Some older beads told us once. If ever you hear the Hand coming, you press yourself hard against the side of the Box, because it's much more unlikely that the Hand will feel right against there. All it usually does is grope about in the middle."

Here Cherry made her tongue and eyes revolve around in imitation of the Hand's movement, which caused a further stream of mirth from all three triplets.

Wheatear had never heard of the trick, but it amazed him far less than the attitude of these three lively, carefree child-beads. They were not very much younger than he was, but they seemed to find fun in everything – even the horrible events of the morning. By pressing themselves against the side, surely they would lessen their chances of being Chosen – but this didn't seem to bother them. Life in or out of the Bead Box – "our Box," they had called it, as if it was their friend – was fun.

Wheatear's heart quickened. He wondered if he could ever be like this. Perhaps he could learn from them. Wheatear was beginning to understand that you can learn something from anyone.

"Come with us and we'll show you where we stay," Robin said. "We'll talk about all sorts of things."

Jostling and jumping, the triplets led the way like small scarlet sparks into the distance. Wheatear followed, full of gladness. Joyfully he looked forward to the time ahead in their company.

As he went, he glanced back over his shoulder to take a last look at the place where they had met. His smile shrank on his lips.

Lurking in the gloom, his eyes fixed on Wheatear like two lamps under murky water, stood the scarred, disfigured body of Amber.

CHAPTER 6:
FRIENDS AND THE DEEPS

Two nights had passed since Wheatear had stared with horror into the eyes of Amber. He had managed to turn his back and continue following his three new friends – although something had altered inside him, and a weight seemed to have sunk to the bottom of his throat.

He had felt those pale, luminous eyes burning like sulphurous beams into his wooden back. The memory of it still made his polish crinkle. But the constant company of the triplet beads almost erased the incident from his mind. Robin, Pippin and Cherry had quickly included him in their team. Their welcome had touched him.

Despite this, somehow he didn't feel ready to tell them about Pebble and Rough. They were so young, so happy, it seemed wrong to dampen their pleasure with talk of his problems. And he feared that they would not understand; he sensed that they felt things with less depth than he did, or perhaps less pain. They had each other. Their bounciness was infectious, but at times Wheatear ached for the contrast of Pebble's more serious, mature conversation.

Yet, when he thought like this, he grew angry with himself. He refused to find any fault with his three red companions, and was in truth very fond of them. They never left him out, or made him feel like a spare part. Twice they had introduced him to their own friends.

Wheatear had grown to think that a good way to tell what beads were like was to look hard at the friends they had. (He felt very wise when he had thoughts like this.) He had looked hard, and listened carefully to the triplets' friends – and he liked them.

First he had met Bee. Bee was a sharp, lively black and yellow bead with a funny little screwed-up face which always made Wheatear want to smile. She was not striped like a bee – she was spotted – but Bee seemed a good name anyway, because of her colours. Anyway, Wheatear was glad that Bee was not striped, because stripes now always reminded him of Mellow. (Or Melon, he noted to himself.) He knew it was unfair on other striped beads to think like that, but he couldn't help it.

Then he had been introduced to Velvet. Velvet fascinated Wheatear, because he was the deepest possible purple – so mysteriously deep that, sometimes, just looking at Velvet made Wheatear feel himself swaying forwards as if he was falling into a hole.

Velvet's features could barely be seen, which gave him an added enigma. His surface was so smooth that it shone like glass, reflecting every tiny glimmer of light that made its way in from the Crack. It often carried the distorted patterns and colours of nearby beads, making Velvet very beautiful. No-one was sure where he came from, and the rising and falling cadences of his voice showed that English was not his first language. He called Wheatear "Veetear."

But by far the most interesting new encounter Wheatear had was with a bead called Lupin. When Wheatear had seen him, a sudden memory had struck him – and when he had heard his name, his heart had jumped. There was no mistaking who this bead was. He was slippery and dark, though not of the lustrous depth of Velvet, and he was long – longer than any bead Wheatear had ever seen. This was who Amber had talked about when he had told the horrifying tale of the bead who slipped down to the bottom of the Bead Box as if through quicksand, and was lying there still.

But Lupin was not lying there still. He was here, with the others.

Wheatear was a little wary of Lupin. His face was right at the top of his long, thin body, and he had a slightly gloomy expression. He was much older than any of Wheatear's other friends. But Wheatear felt he must find out why and how Lupin was not still in the Deeps. He thought Lupin might think he was rude if he asked. It might be touching on a very distressing subject. He tried to think of a suitable and polite way of asking.

Each evening, all the beads met. Humans tend to stick together after a shared disaster; these beads did the same, for they were grateful that they had not become separated as so many friends had. All of them had heard of the trick of pressing against the side of the Bead Box when the Hand came down – "I am pushing till I am feeling I am ze pancake," Velvet said – all except Wheatear, of course. But Wheatear was not upset by this; in his mind was the tiny spark of hope that, if all these beads had heard of it, then surely Pebble and Rough had heard of it too.

The group of beads made a dazzling collection. The three berry-bright dots of scarlet contrasted strongly with the sombre jet body of Lupin. Bee's vibrant yellow, keen as mustard, danced among the spots of black which decorated her – and her pattern and the vivid rosiness of the triplets were all reflected in the soft glossy sheen of Velvet's surface.

On one of these evenings, after a little conversation, there was a pause – and Wheatear's heart quickened.

He had been waiting for such a chance to put his question to Lupin – but now the chance had come, he was filled with such nervous eagerness that he forgot the polite questions he had planned. Instead, he blurted out:

"How come you're not still in the Deeps?"

He stopped in shock at his own voice. Whatever would Lupin think?

But his worries were interrupted by a long, slow noise from the towering bead.

"Hmmmmmmm!" Lupin said in an interested tone. "And how come you know I was ever there?"

Lupin's voice was deep and cultured. He opened his eyes very wide and looked all the way down to where the tiny brown bead sat. His face wore a quizzical expression, but it was not at all unkind.

Wheatear took courage. Haltingly, falteringly, he began to tell how he had been left alone in the Bead Box, and how Amber and Mellow had told him of many terrifying incidents which happened to beads they had heard of or knew. He told how those stories had frightened him, and how Amber had said that Lupin was a good mate of his who slipped down to the Deeps because of his long body ("your unique shape," was how Wheatear phrased it, which he felt was very diplomatic), never to be recovered.

All the time he was speaking, Wheatear did not dare lift his eyes to the far-away face of Lupin – but he was aware that all the assembled beads were listening to him intently.

Finally his words stumbled to a halt.

Lupin was silent for a while, and Wheatear kept his eyes downcast. Then there was a sudden intake of breath from far above him, and he glanced up. Lupin was staring straight ahead with a fixed expression.

"I was *not* a 'good mate' of Amber's," he said, as if he had a deep distaste for the term. "In fact, your story – which I have no reason to disbelieve – makes me even more certain of my opinion of him. I'm afraid I mistrust him. He always, I regret to say, seemed – shifty. Yes: *shifty*."

"I am not knowing this word 'shifty'," Velvet whispered.

"As if he had something to hide," supplied Bee.

Wheatear thought of "Hong Kong" and made a small choking noise.

"Are you all right?" Lupin asked, quickly looking downwards – and after the little bead hastened to reassure him, he went on: "Yes – I don't like him, I'm afraid. No. No."

"I am sorrow to say I am not liking him also," Velvet said. "I sink I am knowing this bead who is resembling the fat drop of the cooking oil. Vonce I see and I say 'Hello,' but to this wording he tell me to become lost. I say to his friend who is stripèd, 'It is fine day.' How-over, she is not in agreement."

Lupin looked downwards and cleared his throat on a long exhalation, murmuring, "Oh dear. Oh dear." He drew himself up slightly. "How-over – er, *however* – allow me to tell you the *true* version of the story..."

Lupin's lofty figure loomed high above them, so that the beads had to strain backwards to keep their eyes on the face of the speaker.

"Would it help if I lay down?" Lupin asked. "It may ease your discomfort."

The beads assented and waited politely while Lupin lowered his lanky frame into a horizontal position.

"I did sink to the depths when I was quite young," he began, "but, contrary to Amber's opinion, I do not lie there still."

He told his listeners that, after recovering initially from the experience of slipping downwards, he – with great strength and will, and also with very welcome help – fought his way up to the Lower Middles – "rather like a *worm*," he boomed, which made Wheatear want to laugh very loudly (though he did not).

"I did not attempt to get any higher up," Lupin went on lugubriously, "for I was by this time so scraped and exhausted I felt it hardly worth the effort. You see, even if I were to have gone higher, I was so scratched that my chances of being Chosen were few and far between." He sighed heavily.

"You don't look too scratched," Wheatear said politely.

Lupin surveyed himself. "My dark colour hides most of it," he said.

"Aren't you ever afraid of sinking to the depths again?" Wheatear asked after a pause.

"Ah," said Lupin. "I'm older now. I am prepared. If ever I feel the slightest shifting from beads below me, I lie down – so." He indicated his horizontal position. "But were I to sink again, I know that help would be at hand – oh... if you'll pardon the rather unfortunate expression."

The beads tried not to think of the word "Hand".

"Please – will you tell me about the Deeps?" Wheatear begged. A horrible fascination urged him to find out more about them.

Lupin yawned massively, and Wheatear saw that the inside of him was as dark as the outside. "I told you I am old," he said, half apologetically. "I fear I am in need of forty, or possibly forty-five, winks. But you have my word that I will tell you about them tomorrow."

With that, his eyes settled shut, and the younger beads, leaving him to his rest, rolled quietly away.

Wheatear passed the night and most of the next day in a fever of impatience. Robin, Cherry, and Pippin chattered and giggled and played harmless games – one of their favourites was rolling down the body of any large bead that would stay still long enough to let them – but Wheatear could think of nothing else but the coming evening and Lupin's promise.

He didn't quite understand the reason for the strange primeval feeling which always stirred within him whenever the Deeps were mentioned. He supposed it was some instinctive urge to horrify himself – the same urge that had forced him to remain and listen to Amber's ghastly stories, when he could have gone away and done something much pleasanter. The very word, 'Deeps' – long, low, hollow – seemed to set a pulse of tingling curiosity beating in his wood.

But the fact remained that, as the light from the Crack gradually diminished, Wheatear became more hoppy and fractious, and kept asking the three beadlets if they didn't think it was time to go to the appointed meeting place. When finally they did decide it was time, they seemed to amble there with agonising slowness – delaying for giggling and shrieking while playing a game they called 'Dodge the Hand' on the way.

Eventually the whole group was once more assembled for an evening chat – although for Wheatear it was a much more important occasion. As Lupin again prepared to speak to them in a prone position, Wheatear felt a tingling in his wood.

The beads gathered round in a circle. (This is a natural position for beads who have been used to being on a necklace or bracelet, and makes them feel at their most comfortable.)

"The Deeps," announced Lupin sonorously – and the words seemed to echo like a bell lost for aeons at the bottom of the sea.

"...which is what our young friend Wheatear wants to hear about," Lupin added in a completely ordinary voice, inclining his head towards the thrilled brown bead. "Wheatear is probably interested in the Deeps for the same reason that others are, which is that they think beads from the Deeps are different from the rest of us. They are."

A prickling feeling of anticipation seemed to crackle in the darkness.

"All those who live in the Deeps," Lupin went on, "are there for a certain reason. Many, for instance, are so small that they have slipped over time through the many spaces between their friends. They are the dwarf beads."

Wheatear almost gasped. He had never imagined such things. No bead that he had ever known had been small enough to pass through the tiny spaces formed between the bodies of others without even disturbing them.

Bee must have been thinking the same thing. "Oo-er," she breathed, crinkling her nose in incredulity. "You mean they're even smaller than the triplets?"

Everyone turned to look at Robin, Pippin and Cherry. The triplets were uncharacteristically silent; their faces had turned from their usual scarlet to a deep crimson, and their eyes were almost as big as their bodies.

"My dear Bee," Lupin said, like a headmaster addressing a very silly pupil, "the bodies of dwarf beads are *minute*. Compared with them, our three friends here are positively *giants*."

The word 'giants', applied to the three tiny rowan-berry blobs forming part of the circle, seemed so incongruous that everybody laughed. Robin, Pippin and Cherry swelled their little chests out as if proud of their new stature. It did much to ease the tension.

"This giant jokings is making me very undistressed," Velvet said, which caused more laughter.

"The dwarf beads, of course," Lupin continued more seriously, "will never get back up again permanently. They can get everywhere, but they will always slip back down. They know that. They accept it, and make a life for themselves down there."

"Are they all small, then, in the Deeps?" questioned Wheatear.

"Not at all. Not at all," said Lupin. "Some beads are there for quite other reasons – because they don't fit in, in some – *other* way." An indefinable look seemed to flit momentarily over his face – but it passed as quickly as it had come. "In fact," he said, lowering his voice a little, "the biggest bead in the entire Bead Box lives in the Deeps."

A faint worry went through Wheatear. He had no

guide to follow as to how big this 'biggest bead' was. He vaguely imagined some monstrous thing lurking and waiting. "How – how big is it?" he quavered.

"Longer than me and five times as broad," Lupin said sceptically, "so I'm told. I wouldn't have thought there was anyone much longer than I in the Bead Box," he added, a little rebuffed.

"This bead makes really the giant," Velvet remarked with interest. "Never are you seeing him?"

"No," Lupin said. "Few beads are actually allowed. He fell down there years ago simply because of his own weight. He just couldn't hold himself up, you know. He really is extremely old. He is also very wise, and it is a great honour to be called into his presence."

"What's his name?" Pippin enquired.

"He is known as the Venerable Bead," Lupin said, "and the dwarf beads and others act as his servants. He is said to be rather a recluse – but that could be because he is getting so old."

"Is he – a Nantique?" Wheatear asked. He had been told this word once, and enunciated it with care.

"Indeed he is an antique, Wheatear," Lupin said, turning again to him. "The Venerable Bead is Venetian millefiori glass, and he is probably very valuable. He has certainly proved himself valuable to many a bead who has come upon trouble. His wisdom has helped many to a better life. Maybe that is why he is reclusive. He needs his privacy – he cannot be expected to help every bead in the Box. I would love to meet him, if only to say thank you."

Everyone had been wondering what 'millefiori' meant, but they now had a more urgent question. Bee voiced it.

"Did he help you, then?" she asked respectfully.

"Not personally, no," Lupin replied. "But he heard of my plight through the dwarf beads – they can get everywhere and then report back – and he sent stronger beads to assist my upward journey."

"Are there lots of strong beads down there?" Robin asked.

"Oh, they didn't just come from the Deeps," Lupin said. "The Venerable Bead has workers in all layers – he hears of them through his beadvine, you know. It wasn't just Deepers who helped me up from the Deeps. I will always be deeply grateful – oh... if you'll pardon the rather unfortunate expression."

Later, in the dark, Wheatear dwelt on what he had heard before he slept. There were a lot of strange things in the world, he decided. He wondered what the future next held for him, and hoped it might be something good.

CHAPTER 7:
VERITY

The pleasant days slipped easily by, and Wheatear could no longer remember how long he had stayed with the triplet beads whose lives were spent in innocent fun and who always managed to make him feel better about things. He would have been very happy indeed, if it had not been for the ever present gnawing anxiety he felt over Pebble and Rough.

He had not yet mentioned them to anyone, as he still felt unable to talk about emotional things with Robin, Pippin and Cherry. He could perhaps have talked to Lupin about his two old friends, or to Velvet – but he never saw Lupin or Velvet alone.

He decided it was best to keep his worries to himself, for he was a private little bead.

During these contented days, he almost forgot his old way of life, but at night the memories of his early time in the Bead Box haunted him, and he missed Pebble sorely. If he suffered a particularly distressing night, he was always glad when morning came; there would be his friends to see and talks to share.

Sometimes Wheatear went for a small explore on his own. When he did, he would try to observe other beads very carefully, as he imagined Pebble would do. But he was always too shy to look them right in the face. He would keep his eyes down and just peep up now and again.

Occasionally on these short rolls he would see Amber. When this happened, both parties simply avoided each other. Wheatear was glad of this, and assumed that Amber, like himself, wanted to forget their past involvement.

Often, in the evenings, if Lupin was tired, the younger beads would sit in a circle chatting amongst themselves. Wheatear liked these times. Sometimes the triplets and Bee made Wheatear feel rather old, but he sensed that Velvet felt the same, and grew fond of Velvet's reliable nature and soft, amiable voice.

A favourite topic for these discussions was the possibility of being Chosen, and on one particular evening their conversation again turned to it.

"For me zere is the advantage and disadvantage to be Chosen," Velvet had just said. His vocabulary was often better than his grammar.

"Good things and bad things," murmured Wheatear.

The beads momentarily looked at him and then back at Velvet.

"Vhat I am meaning is, if we are Chosen, we are having to leave each other. This is causing desolate sorrowness. It is to be saying goodbye to friends."

"Unless we all got threaded together," Cherry giggled.

"That would be extremely unlikely," Lupin said. "For a start, the laws of probability are against it –"

"– and can you honestly see us lot heaped together on one necklace?" Pippin crowed.

The vision of themselves, such a motley crew, attempting to make some sort of hobbledehoy piece of beadwork – large, small, spotted – caused them all (especially Bee and the triplets) such shrieks of mirth that nothing further could be said for a while.

"The Hand usually searches out beads that go together in some way," Lupin continued when the riotous rolling and squeaking had subsided.

"I don't think I'd go with anybody," Bee said in her strange squeaky voice, wrinkling up her sharp little nose.

"You wouldn't match anybody, perhaps," Lupin said, "but you might complement them in some way. The Hand tends to seek beads that have something in common – perhaps the size for example, or the colour scheme, or the material of which they're made."

At this point Wheatear voiced something that had been of interest to him for some time.

"I'm made of wood," he said, "and I'm sure that wood is a very common material for beads. But so far I haven't met a single other bead in the Box that's made of it too."

"Veetear, you are never meeting Verity?" Velvet asked – and immediately Bee and the triplets chorused in apologetic surprise:

"He hasn't met Verity! We should have brought

Verity!"

"Who is Verity?" Wheatear enquired with guarded interest.

"Verity is made by the wood," Velvet said. "Of the wood," he corrected himself.

"She came from a very beautiful bracelet," Robin said impressively.

"She is very special," Cherry said proudly.

"Well I'm sure she wasn't Chosen," said Bee, "because she knows about heading straight for the side. We really must introduce her to Wheatear."

"Would you like to meet her, Wheatear?" Cherry attempted to ask – except it came out as "Would you like to wheat her, Meatear?" and the triplets and Bee went off into paroxysms of laughter yet again.

Velvet and Lupin rolled their eyes wearily and told them to calm down – or rather Lupin did, while Velvet asked them to "be making please the silence".

Wheatear didn't mind, because it gave him time to think. He was still rather shy about meeting new beads. But he liked all these ones, and trusted them. And he would be glad to see another wooden bead – even if it was far more beautiful than himself, plain and brown as he was. In his opinion, he looked like a toasted pip. He supposed that Verity might be larger, and richly carved – perhaps mahogany, or some other precious wood. He suddenly felt rather small.

"If she would like to meet me," he answered timorously.

"Of course she would," Bee said firmly. "It's settled, then. I'll go and find her tomorrow, and bring her along for a chat."

Bee met Wheatear the next morning. She had already been to see Verity, who was to come that afternoon. Verity had said she would be delighted to see them all again, and particularly to meet another wooden bead.

Wheatear was rather worried by the idea of meeting this new personality, especially as he imagined she would probably have cause to look down on him. Her name did not help him to prepare for the meeting. Most beads' names were chosen to match their appearance, but this one gave no clue as to what its owner might look like.

As the time of her arrival approached, Wheatear became more nervous still. He was so settled now with his new friends, he did not want anyone rolling in to spoil it. He had to admit this, even though he knew it was a very selfish attitude.

When afternoon came, he made his way to the meeting place a little early. He had a special reason for doing this. He knew that Velvet was always very punctual, and he particularly wanted to look at his reflection in Velvet's surface before the newcomer appeared. Bouncing self-consciously, he awaited Velvet's arrival.

As he peered into the distance, a gentle, unknown voice came from behind him.

"Have I come to the right place?"

Startled, Wheatear spun round. Then his lips fell open.

Standing before him was the prettiest little bead he had ever seen. She was exactly the size and shape of Wheatear, and was made of the same wood as himself. She was a delicate pink colour and, like Wheatear, had a distinctive wood grain that followed the shape of her neat, round body.

But the most special thing about her was that she was decorated with the most beautiful tiny white flowers, scattering her pink surface like blossoms that dapple a path.

So different was this little bead from Wheatear's image of the coming visitor that, for a few seconds, he was shocked into silence.

Then hastily he remembered his manners.

"I think you must be Verity," he said. "If you are, then you have come to the right place."

The little bead laughed. "And if I'm not?" she said, her eyes twinkling.

Wheatear did not know how to answer this question. It threw him into confusion.

"Well – you're still very welcome anyway," he said politely.

As he spoke, he noticed Verity's ears. They were

quite large – exactly as big as his. He had always been self-conscious about the size of his ears, but on Verity they looked perfect.

The little bead laughed again. "I'm sorry," she said, "that wasn't fair. I am Verity. And as you're made of wood like me, I think you must be Wheatear."

In an agony of self-reproach, Wheatear realised that he had not introduced himself. He babbled an incoherent apology.

"Oh, that's all right," said Verity. "I guessed at once who you are. Look, here come the others."

Out of the soft afternoon light loomed the tall figure of Lupin, fighting off the bobbing forms of the triplets who were leaping around him and begging him to let them ride on his head. Behind them came Velvet and Bee, in conversation. Wheatear felt momentarily annoyed with Bee for keeping Velvet from arriving early enough for him to inspect himself in his surface, but the feeling quickly passed.

"My dear *Verity*," said Lupin in a respectful voice – and, lowering his great frame, he stooped and kissed her.

"Hi there, Verity! Verity, it's us!" chorused the high-pitched voices of Robin, Pippin and Cherry as they scrambled around her.

"Don't knock me over, you scarlet rascals!" Verity said between laughs, backing away from the onslaught and then accepting a kiss from each of them. "Hello, dear Velvet and Bee. It really is lovely to see you all again."

She used ordinary expressions as if she really meant them, thought Wheatear. He stood back from all the greetings, rather awkwardly.

"Wheatear and I have already met," Verity said, including him immediately. "Now let's all have a really good *talk*. I love talking to good friends – don't you, Wheatear?"

Wheatear smiled a little, half in surprise. There was nothing he loved more than talking to good friends, but he would never have actually said so. He would have felt embarrassed. But Verity just said what she felt, and there was nothing embarrassing about it at all.

The afternoon was spent in eager conversation. Verity was a good listener as well as a keen talker. Her company was delightfully refreshing. She could be bubbly when it would add to the mood, but she was calm and serious when it was appropriate.

Wheatear found himself laughing more than he had ever laughed before. Verity made all the beads laugh – a range of sounds, from Bee's little sniggery snort to Lupin's infectious bellow.

Verity was supposed to have left early that evening, but she and everyone else felt loathe to break up the party. As darkness gathered, their voices became quieter and the bright reflections in Velvet's deep violet sides became more muted. Sometimes the beads simply sat, enjoying the amicable silence.

Wheatear felt completely relaxed, and a warm appreciation filled him. As the evening drew on, Verity spoke a little of her past life Outside on her beautiful bracelet. It was not an unusual story: her bracelet had become worn and discarded, and she had found herself in the Bead Box, saved only because her pattern was not rubbed off. She was about the same age as Wheatear, and the small brown bead could sense the hurt in her warm voice; he knew she missed her old life as much as he missed his.

A steady feeling had been growing in Wheatear all the evening, and now he was certain of what he wanted to do. He wanted to tell Verity about Pebble. Her story had made all the old sadness well up in him, and he was sure that, out of all the beads he now knew and trusted, she was the one who would really understand.

CHAPTER 8:
WHAT WOULD HURT YOU MOST

The next few weeks passed in a haze of bliss for Wheatear. After the success of his last conversation with Verity, the beads made a point of inviting her to gather with them whenever she felt like it, which she usually did once every two or three days. Wheatear was by no means the only one who found joy in her company, but for him she held a special significance; it was with Verity that he had felt able to talk about Pebble.

Once he had decided that he would like to tell her about him, Wheatear was a little unsure of how to broach the subject. There was no real problem about seeing her alone; the beads kept no definite time for their meetings, but would simply turn up at the gathering place in the evening if they felt like a chat.

Sometimes Lupin would be too tired to attend, and the others would meet without him. Sometimes Bee was busy elsewhere, or the triplets or Velvet or Verity were not present. But Wheatear went every evening, because he knew there would always be at least one other who would come along too. And then later, before he slept, Wheatear could dwell on the enjoyable conversation – whether it had been a reflective one with Lupin, an effervescent one with Bee, or a companionable one with Velvet. He decided that the next time he and Verity found themselves alone at the meeting place, he would tell her about his missing friend.

It was a week before his chance came.

Of course Rough was missing too, though Wheatear felt more confident that Rough could look after himself (and, to be truthful, was less likely to have been Chosen). Wheatear's greatest and unspoken fear was the vision of the Hand homing in on Pebble's beautiful blue surface – an image he tried to ban from his brain.

He found Verity sitting alone, looking rather

disappointedly about her. Wheatear had deliberately waited until rather late to make sure that no other beads were going to arrive, and this time his patience had been rewarded. When the little flowered bead caught sight of Wheatear, her face broke into a smile of recognition and gladness.

"Oh – Wheatear!" she said warmly. "I thought no-one else was coming tonight. I was just about to go."

"I'm glad you didn't," Wheatear replied, sitting beside her. For many days, Wheatear had puzzled over how to introduce the subject of Pebble; now that his chance had arrived it became a real worry to him. He so desperately needed to tell Verity about his concerns for his friend. He had kept his worries inside for so long, but he didn't want simply to offload his problems on to her. As he was struggling for the best way to begin, Verity said:

"Do you remember when I told you about my life Outside? I don't know anything about yours, Wheatear. I'm always interested to hear about other wooden beads. Where were you before you came here?"

Wheatear's wood seemed to give way like

floodgates released, and he poured out the many memories which had been pent up inside him. Verity listened in silence as Wheatear moved through his story, encouraging him to bring out details which he had thought would not be necessary.

She seemed interested in everything he said, even though he had come from a very modest plain necklace which had been donated to a charity shop. She murmured understandingly when he described how lonely he had felt on his first few nights in the Bead Box; she smiled at how Pebble had been so supportive; she laughed when Wheatear tried to imitate Rough's gruff Cockney voice. And she showed genuine sympathy when he finally told her how, because of the Hand, he had become separated from his two friends.

The two beads talked well into the night. Neither needed to tell the other, but both knew that a special bond was forming between them that had not been there before.

As they parted, Verity said, "We must talk again, Wheatear. Apart from with the others in the evenings, I mean. Could you come here some afternoons? We could meet here, and there'd be no-one else."

"I'd be More Than Happy," answered Wheatear. "Truly."

So it was agreed. Every few days the two little wooden beads met before the light from the Crack had started to fade, and together they would talk – enjoying to the full the unlooked-for gift of each other's company.

But someone else was watching who did not share their sunny laughter or enjoy their growing friendship. Deep in the afternoon shadows, his face curled with hatred of their happiness, the slow yellow eyes of Amber saw all that took place.

Amber was a bead who held a permanent grudge against life. He tried to forget his nightmare journey from Hong Kong, for weeks almost suffocated in plastic wrapping in the freezing hold of a ship, with countless identical beads which on arrival had been used to make key fobs. Some of these went into party crackers, but Amber's fob was displayed with many others on a brightly coloured card in a newsagent's window. The price at which they had retailed was so low that he never liked to think of it.

When, after many months, the card in the window began to fade and his key fob had still not been purchased, he had swung and fought and rubbed on the cheap thread which joined him to his fellows; he had flung himself on the floor of the shop, well away from the others, and had hidden behind a pile of undelivered newspapers.

One hot day, when the door of the shop was propped open, he had rolled out on to the street so that he would never be reunited with the rest of the key ring's beads.

He had been picked up, dropped in the Bead Box, called himself Amber, and from that moment pretended that was what he was. But, all the time, he knew he would never be what he wanted to be. He lived with a bitter loathing of the stamp he carried, and thought that if he kept it hidden he could maintain the pretence of greatness and win some high-class friends.

But when someone continually tries to pretend that they are better than they are, and never admits that they have any faults, they don't make many real friends – and that is what had happened to Amber. Most beads despised him; many feared him; a few pitied him. It grieved Amber sorely to see beads less beautiful than he considered himself to be, such as Rough, making friends for themselves with no difficulty. Rough, though, had been a useful ally – big and tough. Amber had worked hard to get into Rough's circle.

Wheatear he loathed deeply. The real truth was that Amber was jealous, but he would not admit this to himself. Whenever the idea came to his mind, he would snap to himself in anger that Wheatear was a blubbering fool, a babyish pathetic creature, as dull and plain as any bead could be. He hated Wheatear for turning up when he had – Amber reckoned he was just beginning to get in with Rough when this stupid, whimpering weakling had turned up to claim all the attention.

And Rough stuck up for him, Amber raged inwardly. *Stuck up for that ordinary, brown, big-eared bobble! All I did*, he thought sulkily, *was frighten the silly little idiot with a few old horror stories – but I paid for it all right.*

He looked down bitterly at his scarred stomach. If

only it had been a bit lower down, the knock might have scraped off the hated stamp. Why couldn't it have happened that way?

Because I don't go waving that bit of me around for all to see, Amber thought impatiently. *And anyway; nothing ever happens the way I want it.*

As it was, Amber knew that he was disfigured for life, and for this he blamed neither himself nor Rough. Rough, he knew, had acted in self-defence, and bore the marks of more than one fight. That was just Rough's way. Rough wasn't a bead of many words – not much intelligence there, Amber reckoned – and probably didn't realise his own strength. No: it was that whining Wheatear that had brought all this about.

The desire for revenge had burned in Amber ever since the incident had taken place. And now that he had been lucky enough after the Hand's visit to find himself still near to Wheatear, but without Rough to interfere, this desire brewed and boiled ever more dangerously.

Most of all, Amber hated the friendship that Wheatear and Verity shared. As time went by he had watched it developing. To see the prettily petalled, pinkly perfect bead listening to Wheatear's every word, to hear their easy laughter, was maddening to Amber. The lust for revenge rose ever higher within him.

Noting that several beads had come to Rough's assistance when he and Mellow had 'surprised' him (as he termed it in his mind), Amber had, over the last few weeks, gathered together a new and particularly unsavoury gang of beads which he had singled out as having certain similarities. They all found themselves newly stranded without friends, they were all less than gracious in moral character, and they all harboured some bitterness towards life in general.

Amber had also made certain that they would all obey him as a leader, for it was noticeable that without exception the beads he had chosen were all smaller than himself. With this posse he held meetings at dead of night, which were similar to those of Wheatear and his friends – except that, at Amber's meetings, each bead endeavoured to outdo the others in the nastiness of their chosen topics.

But they were all obliged to agree, when the meeting broke up, that the nastiest tales of all had been Amber's. If they didn't, he would grow mad with rage – and all the next day he would sulk.

The gang always did his bidding. They dared not disagree with him. One of Amber's chief delights at these midnight gatherings was to boast about how he had terrified Wheatear by telling him horror stories. He always chuckled when he recalled this, and told his favourite little snippets again. His gang members were obliged to laugh each time too.

But lately Amber seemed to have given up the topic of how he had upset Wheatear in the past. He now seemed more interested in what he might do to upset him in the future.

And that week he had hit on it. At the next meeting, Amber and his cronies talked as usual in the thick, impenetrable night. But on this occasion the meeting was punctuated with more chuckling than usual, Amber's throaty whisper held a particularly eager note, and at one moment he roared with horrible mirth.

Meanwhile, unknowing and far away, Wheatear and his companions slept the sleep of the innocent. All except one. Somewhere, closer than Amber knew or dreamed of, hiding in the blackness, one single bead was listening.

The following evening, none of Wheatear's friends met at the common meeting place to pass the time away in pleasant chat. Earlier that day, Bee had brought Wheatear a message telling him instead to come as soon as he judged it was night. The friends were to meet only when it was pitch dark and at no other time, she said. When Wheatear asked why this was, Bee looked worried and said she didn't know – but that was what she'd been told to pass on. Before Wheatear could question her further, Bee, looking anxiously about her, had buzzed off into the gloom.

Wheatear passed the day in uneasy perplexity. He would have given almost anything to have talked to one of his friends, especially Verity, but he dared not search for anyone because of Bee's message – which had seemed to carry a note of warning. To Wheatear, meeting only at the dead of night sounded sinister. He did nothing very much all day but roll around aimlessly around near the same spot, willing the time to pass.

When the light began to diminish, Wheatear worried about just how dark he should wait for it to be. He didn't like the idea of going alone to the meeting in complete blackness, but he didn't want to arrive early because he had a vague feeling that it might be dangerous. He waited, searching around for some clue as to what might be happening.

Some time later he awoke with a start. Someone was buffeting him, bustling him along. He blinked his eyes, then stretched them wide open, but he could see nothing.

A voice below his straining eyes hissed, "Here he is! Fancy being asleep!"

Another small voice on his other side said,

"Come *on*, Wheatear. It's dark! You dozed off."

"Whu– who?" mumbled Wheatear indistinctly.

"It's Robin and Cherry," one of them whispered. "Now *come on*. The others are waiting."

Now fully alert, Wheatear felt greatly ashamed that he had let the others down by failing to keep awake till darkness fell. But he did not stop to apologise, because he had caught the urgency in the two little beads' voices – a worrying contrast to their usual jollity. Robin and Cherry hustled him along to the meeting place, only a few beadrolls from where he had slept.

The darkness was darker than Wheatear had imagined that darkness could be. He sat anchorless, as if sinking in a lake of ink, unable to guess his position. Even the thrum was faint, though it was never entirely still. It seemed to tremble distantly from far below.

"Greetings, Wheatear," came a low tone – causing Wheatear to jump and stare into the blackness far above him. It was Lupin's hushed voice. "We are glad you have come. Pippin has much to tell us."

"Hurry to be telling us this news, Peepeen," Velvet urged softly, from somewhere to Wheatear's right. "Do not be missing the small tail."

"Detail," hissed Bee.

In a steady, high-pitched whisper, the voice of Pippin came from across the circle as he told his story. He had been for a gentle roll on the previous evening by himself ("to get some peace away from these two," he joked, for which he was nudged sharply by his siblings), and had spotted Verity and Wheatear talking. Seeing that they were deep in conversation, and not wanting to interrupt, he had smiled at them, but they had not noticed him.

Just as he was about to pass by, he had caught a glimpse of someone else who was also looking in their direction. A big, bruised bead – like a fat blob of treacle – with a look in his eyes that had made Pippin stop.

"Amber." The word dropped almost inaudibly from Wheatear's mouth.

Pippin went on to tell how he had pretended to be exploring nearby, but had kept watching the expression on Amber's face as Wheatear and Verity continued talking. Once, when they both laughed aloud at something they had said, Amber's look had become particularly menacing.

This had been enough for Pippin. He had decided what to do.

"And what was that?" Bee asked in her squeaky whisper.

"I followed him," Pippin said simply.

There was a short silence.

"That, my dear Pippin, was an extremely dangerous thing to do, and I fear you have caused your two siblings much worry." Lupin's voice registered grave concern.

"But I had to," Pippin insisted. "If you'd seen the look on his face, you'd have done the same."

No-one was surprised that not a sound came from either Wheatear or Verity. All the beads were stilled with horror.

"Vhere does he go?" Velvet asked.

Pippin then described how he had discovered

the meeting ground of Amber and his unpleasant associates. When he described the tone of their discussion, something cold dribbled inside Wheatear's throat. He remained unable to speak.

"But how come they didn't see you?" Bee voiced the question in everyone's minds. Pippin was so brightly coloured.

"It was easy," Pippin replied. "I hid inside a big bead's ear. He was asleep, so he didn't feel me."

The silence intensified as everyone took in this information. Wheatear was filled with awe for Pippin's quick thinking and bravery – but other feelings, too, were beginning to stir within him.

"What were they saying?" Robin asked eventually.

"Well, it was quite difficult to hear anything they said," Pippin explained, "because the bead – the one

I was in – was snoring rather loudly. But I did hear quite a bit of it."

"What? It is most important that you tell us," Lupin whispered with urgency.

Pippin repeated all he'd managed to hear – but much of it was only in snatches, gleaned between the snores of the large bead who had unknowingly shielded him. The word 'revenge' had occurred often, usually with sounds of assent and cheering from Amber's gang. Then Amber had said something about "the thing that'll hurt that Pudden most of all."

"I am not knowing this word, 'Pudden'," Velvet said.

"Nor I," Lupin responded. "I confess all this means nothing to me."

Wheatear's wood was beating so thickly that he could hardly breathe, but he found his voice. "It does to me," he said from the darkness.

He felt the beads turn in his direction, and imagined their questioning faces. In a low, almost soundless voice, controlled with some difficulty, Wheatear told them of how he had caused Rough to inflict a wound on Amber many weeks ago, and of the nickname 'Pudden' which it seemed Amber still used for him. A heavy stillness followed his explanation, during which Wheatear's breath quickened and his wood seemed to seize into a hard ball.

Finally Lupin spoke.

"What we have heard is very serious," he said, "and we must now appeal to you, Pippin, to tell us every possible detail of the conversation you witnessed – no matter how irrelevant or unpleasant it may seem."

"Some of it was – not very pleasant," ventured Pippin, "but I see now that I must tell it. The only other thing I heard Amber say was – sorry, Wheatear – 'It'll be an easy matter to push that wide-eared wooden wimp down to the Deeps. No Hand will ever choose a bead from down there.' Then he – he laughed nastily."

"This vide-ear vooden vimp is Veetear," Velvet gasped in alarm.

Wheatear had to agree.

"How are they planning to force him down?" Lupin barked quickly.

"I don't know," Pippin said, racking his brains for the exact memory. "Amber said something like 'lads in each layer,' or words to that effect."

"He's going to position his accomplices all the way down through the layers of the Bead Box," Lupin exclaimed.

"And push you down from one to another. Oh, Wheatear!" Cherry wailed.

"They're bullies, cruel bullies," Bee sobbed.

But Wheatear, instead of feeling the blank horror and terrifying despair that his friends assumed he was feeling, was thinking very hard of something – something that didn't satisfy him; two facts that didn't quite piece together.

His silence worried the beads.

"Veetear is all right?" Velvet said suddenly, and anxious beads felt their way towards him.

"Oh yes, I'm all right," Wheatear said in a strange voice. "It's just that – it doesn't quite make sense. It doesn't fit."

"What doesn't fit?" Lupin asked, reaching his face down to Wheatear's level.

"Well..." Wheatear said slowly. "Pippin heard Amber say he was going to do the thing that would hurt me most of all. And then he said that he would push 'that wide-eared wooden wimp down to the Deeps.'"

"And?" Lupin said, somewhat impatiently.

"Well – it's just that – that isn't what would hurt me most," Wheatear said. "It would frighten me, very much, but it wouldn't hurt me. 'Hurt' seems the wrong word altogether."

Lupin sighed. He did not really see that the choice of word made a great deal of difference.

But Velvet spoke. "Vhat is hurting you most of all, Veetear?" he asked intently.

Wheatear cast his eyes downwards into darkness, and said nothing.

"I sink I am knowing vhat is hurting you the most," Velvet said gently. "It is to be losing Verity, yes? I am right? But you give no speech because you are feeling the shyness to say it in front of her."

The little bead looked down into the black. Even though he made no reply, all the beads knew his answer.

Lupin's voice took on a quickened note. "It is as Wheatear thought," he said. "The pieces don't fit. The 'wide-eared wooden wimp' that Amber and his crew are planning to force down, never to be Chosen, is not Wheatear, but Verity!"

A stunned silence fell like a blow on the assembled

beads. It was broken by a wail from Wheatear.

"Ssh! Do not despair," Lupin hissed. "The main thing is to protect Verity. All gather round her at once."

"Where is she?" asked several voices, as the beads knocked together in the blackness. "Verity! Verity, where are you?"

They stopped shuffling.

"Who is being next to Verity?" Velvet said sharply.

No-one answered his question.

"She's not here!" Robin shouted.

"But she said she was coming!" Bee squeaked desperately.

"She never got here – she never arrived!" Lupin cried. "There is no time to lose! Hurry – we may already be too late!"

CHAPTER 9:
THE PILGRIMAGE

After the discovery of Verity's absence, the beads' first reaction had been a rush of good intent. But they had quickly realised that they had neither the ideas nor the stamina to solve such a problem as this. They were all in need of sleep, they needed light to work by, and most of all they needed to formulate a very careful set of plans to avoid getting into any danger themselves. At that moment their minds had been too anxious to think calmly, and they agreed to spend the rest of the night trying to catch up on the sleep they had lost then meet at the Crack's first light the next day.

When the beads had dispersed, Wheatear sat alone in the meeting place. There he wept for the first time since he had cried with Pebble.

Finally, he heaved a sigh. He decided there was only one thing to do.

He had to go down to the Deeps and find Verity himself.

Fighting down the feelings of terror which mounted in him, Wheatear made his plans. He dared not involve the others. Some of them were so young and small. He also felt he could move less conspicuously on his own. One smallish brown bead passing by would not attract much attention, but a group of seven – especially with distinctive shapes like Lupin's, and brilliant colours like Bee's and the triplets – would soon be remembered.

So how would he get to the Deeps? Just plunge down, as Lupin had, through the bodies of others? The very thought of it made his wood give way. But it also lacked sense. No: he would have to journey, as he had meant to once before, to the side of the Box, and then feel his way down from there, keeping to the side all the time.

Travelling that way, there would be less chance of

being seen and much less of losing his way. He would simply follow the side of the Box down until he could go no further. Then he would be there.

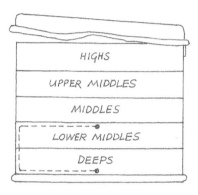

At least, that's what he tried to tell himself. Already he was trembling. He had never been on a journey of this kind, and all he knew of the Deeps was the little that others had told him. He knew that it was possible, even likely, that he would never see his friends again if he went. But if he told them he was going, they would insist on coming with him – or try to stop him. And if he went to say goodbye, he knew he would be so upset that he would never go at all.

Setting his lips in a firm line, he came to the final question in his mind. When should he go? Amber and his gang had held their conversation a day earlier.

But that helped Wheatear very little, as he had no idea how far below the Deeps were – just as he had no idea how far above him his original layer lay. The Hand's visit had left him completely disoriented.

Nor did he know whether Amber had already forced Verity to the Deeps, or whether he had not even started. It was possible, if the Deeps were not too far below, that she was there already.

This decided Wheatear. He had to start now, while it was still dark. He would just keep going till he felt the side. He would soon be there.

With the grain of his wood crawling within him, and his eyes still unable to penetrate the blackness, Wheatear began to roll.

To a bead who had never undertaken any major journey by means of his own power, and especially a bead who was alone, the distance to the side of the Box seemed enormous. Wheatear believed it had become light and pitch black twice more since he began, and still he pressed onwards. Sometimes he really had to think hard to decide whether it was day or night. He had slept, but not to a regular pattern.

He was under strain from the constant possibility of someone asking where he was going, dazed from the constant peering ahead, and sickened by the constant texture of beads' bodies against his own surface. He realised it was almost impossible to roll in a straight line, as he was going round the bodies of beads – or groups of beads – every moment of his journey. For all he knew he could have been travelling in a circle.

It was in this stupefied state when, in absolute darkness for the second time, he hit the side.

It came as a shock because he had not been able to see it – and because, after so long, he had almost expected never to reach it. But now the first step of his journey was achieved.

That night he slept better, giving up his weary wooden body to the rest it so badly needed. As the filtering light woke him the next day, Wheatear examined the side of the Box. He had to know it very well, so as not to lose track of it for one moment on his dangerous vertical pilgrimage. Having thoroughly familiarised himself with the texture of it, the smell of it, and the noise it gave when he knocked against it, Wheatear began to edge himself slowly downwards in the early light.

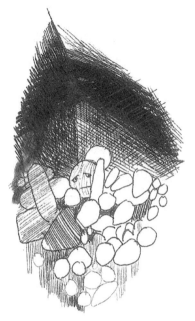

At first he was so terrified of losing contact with the side of the Box that he scraped against it as he went, scratching his once polished surface and making it very sore.

He had begun his journey to the side by saying "Excuse me" to every bead he touched – which meant that he was saying it all the time – but after the first day he had become a more hardened traveller, realising that other beads were less likely to remember him if he didn't speak. Now he saved his breath for pushing himself downwards – a much tougher task than moving along horizontally. A few beads threw him annoyed glances, but moving to one side for an insignificant brown bead was not a memorable occasion, and held no further interest for them.

Darker and darker, deeper and deeper he went, his wood numbed with scratches and the jostling of others. At one stage he almost gave up, convinced that he was sacrificing body and spirit on what might turn out to be a futile journey.

But then he thought of Verity, and continued on his mission.

On the third afternoon, he was wriggling downwards as usual – a movement that had become painfully familiar to him. He pushed his way past a faceted bead, a small orange-coloured bead, a grey clay bead. They had all become faceless to Wheatear – yet more beads out of the hundreds he had passed. Then his body came down against a flattish surface – perhaps a square-shaped or cuboid bead, Wheatear thought. He pushed harder but it would not give way.

"Excuse me," he said finally, looking beneath him.

Then he saw. A shock ran through his wood as he realised he was pressing on a hard, flat area of the same texture as the side of the Box.

His mouth gasped, his eyes fell shut, and he drew a shuddering breath.

He had reached the Deeps.

With the second stage of his journey complete, Wheatear allowed himself to relax a little – and, as he did so, he realised how exhausted he was. Even if he had felt able, he would not have started his search for Verity that night; darkness was closing in fast, and he wanted to gain a good knowledge of his new surroundings so as not go plunging into them recklessly. He was very much on his guard, and he was right to be, for who knew what dangers besides Amber were waiting to greet him? Lupin had said that the beads in the Deeps were different – and Wheatear had a feeling that he hadn't just meant bigger or smaller. 'Different' could mean anything. Was there something else – something he had to be careful about? He remembered how he had felt in his wood the very first time he had heard the Deeps mentioned.

He wedged himself as far into the angle formed by the side and base of the Box as his hard, round body would allow. He knew that sleep was extremely important to prepare for the next day.

He did sleep, but it was a sleep of unease and disquiet, drifting with vague forebodings.

He rose early, awake but not refreshed. He felt his aches and scratches fully now. But he was determined to carry out at least the next stage of his plan as soon as possible.

This was to find any bead who looked responsible and trustworthy, and pluck up the courage to ask where to find the Venerable Bead. It was useless to ask beads if they had seen Verity – although he would ask anyway – for even if they had, she would probably be guarded by Amber or some members of his notorious gang.

No: he needed help, and he was sure that the Venerable Bead would be the most professional help he could get.

Wheatear moved along very cautiously. He was aware that, at any moment, he might stumble upon the very place where Amber was lurking. He skirted the side at first, then dared to venture away from it, his eyes darting in every direction. Often he dodged behind the bulk of some larger bead, especially if he thought he saw something worrying. Once he thought he heard a sinister shuffling, and leapt in terror to the nearest refuge, expecting to see Amber's burly frame bearing down upon him. But he soon learned that, in the Deeps, ordinary rolling made a different noise, because these beads moved on the base of the Box.

He pressed on.

It was darker here than anywhere else in the Bead Box, and Wheatear found it difficult to adjust. At about the time he judged to be late morning, he saw ahead of him a bluish bead, rolling along and staring about her. The colour made Wheatear think of Pebble. He thought he would choose this bead to ask the way. Rolling up to her, he cleared his throat, ready to put a polite question.

Then he stopped.

As the blue bead passed him, Wheatear saw that she had no ears – no hole at all by which to be threaded. She was, in fact, not really a bead at all, but a sort of ball, who must have got thrown in and ended up here.

With new eyes, Wheatear looked around him. A short distance away was a bead so ugly that shock and pity flooded Wheatear. The bead was made of plastic, but something must have been wrong with the mould. It had left a grotesque ridge like a hard, bony plate around his whole body where the two halves joined.

Wheatear wrested his eyes away. These had to be the 'different beads' that Lupin wouldn't talk about. This layer, the Deeps, had become an underworld; a gathering for beads who felt they could not live in other layers because they were too small, too heavy, or did not conform in some other way. Here, it seemed to Wheatear, were the rejected, the disfigured, the gross, the maimed, and probably the evil and the mad. Here were all those from other layers who were too different to be anywhere else: beads hardened with resentment, hurt by injustice, ignored, unheard, unhelped.

And here also, Wheatear thought as he crouched in the vice-riddled gloom, *is Verity.*

It was the next day. Wheatear's demands to know the whereabouts of the Venerable Bead had been met with incredulity, surprised laughter and blank stares. It seemed to Wheatear that few beads knew, cared, or had bothered to find out where the great wise bead lived – or perhaps they thought Wheatear was crazy to imagine that he could speak to him. Their reactions haunted the little bead, whose wood was sickly pale with the stress of his search.

He had heard nothing of Verity.

It was about mid-afternoon when Wheatear decided he could go no further. Weary, lost, and lacking all energy, he slumped beside a pile of small beads, feeling more dejected than he had ever felt in his life.

Aimlessly he stared around him. He saw a purple bead with a distressing surface of peeling paint, as if scabs were lifting all over him. Wheatear was used to such sights now. He would have one more try – he had nothing to lose.

In an expressionless voice he said, "Could you tell me the way to the Venerable Bead?"

The purple bead looked up and stared.

Wheatear's heart sank. Once more the look of disbelief.

"Are you serious?" the purple bead asked.

Wheatear had heard it all before.

But then...

"You couldn't get much nearer," the purple bead shouted as he made off. "You're sittin' at 'is door!"

"Wait!" yelled Wheatear, leaping up. "What did you say?"

The scabrous bead returned slowly. "His door," he repeated, slowly and clearly. "Knock at them beads. An' good luck ter yer!"

Rolling his eyes and shaking his flaking head, the purple bead went on his way.

Wheatear whirled round and surveyed the pile of small beads against which he'd been sitting. For a while he stood still. Then, gingerly, he leaned his body forward and tapped the pile twice.

Instantly the beads separated into two walls, between which a path ran into the darkness.

Wheatear jumped, his heart beating in his throat.

Nothing else happened.

After waiting to see if anything would, Wheatear ventured down the pathway, his own breath audible.

A little way further, he heard a smart, scrunching sound behind him lasting no longer than half a second. Turning in fright, he saw that he was hemmed in. The walls had sealed up behind him, the beads forming their original pile.

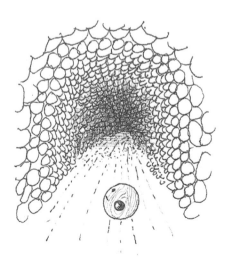

A voice said quickly, "Name, sir?"

Wheatear turned back and saw the strangest glass bead he could ever imagine. It looked as if the glass he was made of had melted and then set before being properly moulded. The bead was irregular in shape, his ear holes distorted, but he puffed his little uneven chest out proudly.

Wheatear gave his name and, in answer to further questions which were efficiently directed at him, explained his reasons for wanting to see the Venerable Bead.

After a close inspection, the glass bead said, "Please come this way."

Wheatear was ushered into a completely unexpected place. It was an opulent chamber, a grotto composed entirely of beads. The curved roof consisted of millions of dwarf beads of all colours, arching in vault-like patterns, supporting themselves on one another. He stared in wonder at their glistening beauty.

"WHO IS THIS SMALL BROWN BEAD?" came a rich, cultured bass voice that made Wheatear whisk round to face the speaker.

Cushioned among his minute minions reclined a vast, weighty, ancient bead – the most elaborate that Wheatear had ever seen. Every colour that could be imagined was represented on his colossal surface in the most intricately designed patterns and swirls, which seemed to change as he shifted his immense body. His beauty and grandeur were beyond anything that Wheatear had expected.

As Wheatear watched, beads of all types moved constantly around their master, attending to his every possible comfort. Some dwarf beads scratched his ears by rolling inside them; stronger ones pushed the beads in the walls and roof into neater positions; a collection of others provided entertainment by forming themselves into ever-changing patterns on the floor around him.

The glass bead who had accompanied Wheatear now positioned himself before the Venerable Bead's throne. "A visitor, Your Excellency," he announced.

"A visitor," repeated His Excellency, leaning forward and opening his remarkably patterned eyes very wide. "*Ma certo*, I can see he's a visitor. What I'd like to know is why he is visiting. Where are you from, you small brown visitor, you young ACORN?"

Righteous indignation filled Wheatear. No matter how wealthy or famous you were, there was no need to be rude. He drew himself up and looked at his questioner.

"Great oaks from little acorns grow, Your Excellency," he said in his clearest, politest little voice.

The Venerable Bead's richly decorated eyes nearly

popped out of his gloriously patterned head. He stared at Wheatear – and then slowly began to look interested. The corners of his mouth twitched and his eyes showed a slight twinkle. "*Piccola ghianda,*" he murmured, and then commanded, "Form a footstool for the little acorn."

Instantly the kaleidoscopic pattern-making beads compressed themselves into a solid mass in the shape of a delicate little buffet, upon which Wheatear daintily sat down. He felt very guilty about sitting on the poor beads.

"Now, where have you come from?" said the Venerable Bead gently.

Wheatear, too concerned about his mission to feel fear, began the tale of his errand of mercy. And when, many hours later, the grotto was sealed in darkness and the dwarf beads were at last released from their labours, it was a very sympathetic listener who began to offer his advice.

CHAPTER 10:

EXCHANGE PLACES

For three days, Wheatear's every need was provided for in the palace, and he was attended constantly by the Venerable Bead's own dwarf bead servants who seemed delighted to be of help. Wheatear was full of admiration for the organised way in which so many were working for him.

The Venerable Bead had proved that his reputation for kindness and wisdom was well founded. After asking where Wheatear had travelled from, he had wanted to know if he had travelled before, and then if he had travelled alone. At Wheatear's answers, he looked grave.

But he still did not ask what Wheatear wanted.

Instead he asked why Wheatear appeared to be so frightened of the Deeps. Wheatear had explained what he had been told, and that Lupin had said that beads here were 'different'. At the name of Lupin, the Venerable Bead had smiled, and asked how 'the dear fellow' was. Wheatear assured him he was well, and taking frequent horizontal naps.

"*Splendido!*" the Venerable Bead boomed in operatic tones, laughing with pleasure. Wheatear had noticed that he occasionally used Italian phrases, although his voice retained no trace of an Italian accent – it sounded as if he had been raised in well-to-do English society. "A good friend to know. And do *you* think the beads down here are 'different'?"

"Oh yes," said Wheatear. "I saw – a blue bead with – no ears – and a purple bead with – with all his paint lifting off, and a bead with sort of a hard plastic edge. It seems so very sad."

"What were these beads doing?" the Venerable Bead asked.

Wheatear thought hard. He had only really noticed what he thought was wrong with them.

"Just going about their business," he replied.

"*Esattamente*," the Venerable Bead said with a smile. "*Precisamente*. Because they all have business to go about. Blueberry is deaf, not sad. She is extremely useful in warning us when the Hand is coming, because she feels the slightest vibration. She can also detect falls and fights in the same way. A wonderful warning system. Grape, the purple chap, is down here while his paint lifts off; he'll go up again when he's finished scraping against the base to clean himself up ready for Choosing. Shovel is marvellous."

"Shovel?" Wheatear questioned.

"The ridged one," the Venerable Bead said. "The moulded shape around his middle is wonderful for shovelling up the smaller beads down here, digging paths, and so on. Such a blessing. Never would have built the palace without him. *Bravo ragazzo!* Champion fellow, loves his work."

The little brown bead was silent for a moment. Then he asked, "Is that what Lupin meant by 'different'?"

"It is," the Venerable Bead said. "We can be different in many ways. 'Different' doesn't have to mean 'bad'. Or 'sad'. Of course, there are *some* sad beads down here, as there are everywhere else in the Bead Box.

And beads who know, perhaps because of their appearance, that they will never be Chosen. But many beads here have no particular wish to be Chosen. They have made fulfilling and contented lives, and they enjoy them. My chief servant is one of them. I wouldn't be without him."

The small brown visitor had a question burning inside him, burning as strongly as when he had wanted to ask Lupin why he was no longer in the Deeps. But he had blurted that question out very rudely. He knew he could not do the same again here. He took a breath, paused, and then said:

"Your Excellency, may I ask... You are so – magnificent! How is it that *you* have never been Chosen?"

The glorious bead before him did not show any sign of offence.

"You are not the first to ask me that question," he said in a practical way. "All my life I have been repeatedly told that I am *bellissimo*, and handled and admired – but only by antique dealers and collectors who wanted to display me behind glass. I love the company of children, but to be with them was something that was never possible for me. I was always told I was too old, too precious for them. I was also too heavy for a necklace. There was an awful moment" – he smiled wryly – "when I was in a bric-a-brac box in an antique shop, and thought my fate was to become a bathroom light pull. Dreadful – *terribile* – I hate both solitude and heights."

Wheatear looked with new eyes at his dazzling host. It had never occurred to him that such a bead's life might actually be very restricted, or that beauty might be a disadvantage. He tried to imagine swinging endlessly and alone on a light pull, repeatedly being grasped by a clutching Hand, going from blinding light to darkness.

He threw the thought away as the Venerable Bead's voice continued.

"Instead of being Chosen, I did the choosing," he said. "I was always drawn to the idea of reducing problems, removing difficulties – helping others, I suppose – and I chose to make a life down here where I can do that, and in return be very comfortably looked after by those I help."

Wheatear pondered on this. He knew, deep in his wood, that what he still passionately wanted was to be Chosen – but he thought how narrow his understanding had been of others' choices.

But the conversation had also made him think of Amber. Amber was not leading a fulfilling, helpful or contented life.

And neither, at the moment, was Verity.

It was then that the Venerable Bead saw that the moment was right. "You have travelled from another layer, you have never travelled before, and you have travelled alone," he said gently, "to a place which filled you with terror. I am guessing it is for an important reason. So, *piccola ghianda* – little acorn – what brings you here?"

Wheatear's story poured out. And, once the Venerable Bead saw that it was genuine, he offered to give Wheatear all the support in his power.

On the morning after their talk, the Venerable Bead commanded a search party of hundreds of dwarf beads to discover the whereabouts of Amber and Verity. Once out of the grotto, the minute beads were to scatter in pairs and creep into every crevice and cranny the Deeps contained. Apparently Pippin's idea of hiding in larger beads' ears was a common ploy well-known to them for years, but they were so much smaller than the triplets that they could hide in even tinier spaces such as the minute fissure between the side and base of the Bead Box, or under a bead's overhanging stomach. Being transparent, they could often stand against a coloured bead without being noticed. They could also group together to camouflage themselves as larger, studded beads. Their ingenuity was remarkable. Wheatear conceded that they would never have such an exciting life on a necklace – though if being in here was an exciting life, he didn't want one.

When the dwarf beads had tracked down their quarry they were to report back immediately – and, for hour upon age-long hour, Wheatear had been waiting. By the next night he had almost given up hope. Surely they should have found her by now!

Perhaps she had never reached the Deeps. Perhaps Amber had done something worse to her. Wheatear shut his eyes tight. He wondered if the mystery would ever be solved at all.

He slept for the second time on a dainty cushion of dwarf beads, his hope decreasing with every minute that passed.

In the middle of the night, he woke. Someone was jogging him, thudding at his wood.

Blinking, Wheatear saw to his amazement that it was His Excellency himself. His huge bulk towered in the gloom.

"They have found her," he said, watching Wheatear's face. "And now I believe there may be challenging work to be done to ensure her safe return. Come."

Shaking with excitement, Wheatear fell from his bed and blundered after the Venerable Bead. As they hurried to the grotto's studded entrance, His Excellency told Wheatear what had already taken place. Apparently one search party had brought news of a flowered pink bead.

"News?" repeated Wheatear. "Did they see her?"

"No," the Venerable Bead replied. "But they were told about her. By a reliable source," he added.

Wheatear was disappointed, but did not like to question further, and in any case the Venerable Bead was now telling him what else had been going on.

It seemed that, on hearing the news, he had called together his army of metal beads: hard, steely, and known for their fearlessness and strength. Wheatear had not known about the existence of this army, but it appeared that their training and bravery as beads were unsurpassed. The army beads, unlike their miniature colleagues, had not separated. Instead they had formed a long line, and were at this moment on alert for a word from their great commander to move in on Amber and his crew.

As the Venerable Bead was explaining this, they exited the palace portals – and Wheatear stopped short.

Arrayed in ranks before him, utterly unmoving and silent, were dozens of shining steel soldier beads, each exactly the same as the next. The effect was of chain mail. It was hard to accept that the gleaming mass was actually composed of single beads. Even their eyes were fixed unblinkingly ahead.

"Let me repeat," the Venerable Bead said to his soldiers in a firm voice. "It is the safety of the bead Verity that is our focus, and we believe she is being held by one who goes by the name of Amber. There may also be others accompanying and obeying him. *No* violence must be used unless absolutely necessary, and you will take no action unless you receive a direct command from me. Forward!"

Wheatear's wood leapt with shock as the army beads drew themselves up smartly and in unison, making a sudden very loud metallic rapping against each other and the base of the Box, and then obeyed their leader with a noise which quickly built into a deafening rattle. Wheatear wondered what on earth Blueberry would make of this level of vibration.

The glinting army undulated like a huge, snake-like battalion of matching steel bullets, moving ceaselessly onwards and forwards as if one creature. Each bead kept contact with the next to form an impenetrable barrier. The floor of the Box rattled; the noise was like a drill.

"Come, Wheatear!" shouted the Venerable Bead. "*Sbrigati!*"

Rolling as fast as he could to keep up with his huge multi-coloured host, Wheatear bumped along, his heart pounding. He had no idea where they were going, whether it was near or far, or what the plan of action might be. They seemed to be heading in a direct line to the side of the Box. Any further, and surely they would reach the wall.

And then he saw Amber.

Stuck like a lump of toffee to the spot, Amber's unlovely face held its cruel, menacing expression.

Wheatear stopped as relentlessly the army moved forward. It darted through his mind that neither the

Venerable Bead nor the army had set eyes on Amber before. He needed to tell them.

There was a ringing in his ears. His throat dry as parched wood, a cracked sound escaped his lips as he tried to warn them.

But the Venerable Bead already seemed to know. Without yelling, he called clearly, "Halt!" There was a stunning silence as the army stopped instantly. Then, to the hostile bead, he said, "Amber, please stand aside."

Wheatear could hear Amber breathing. He could vaguely make out some smaller shape, distorted like a funfair mirror, through the parts of Amber that still had some transparency. And then, slowly, Amber moved his treacly yellow bulk to one side – revealing the small, terrified figure of Verity.

Wheatear felt as if something wide was expanding up through his throat to choke him.

Quietly, the Venerable Bead moved towards him. "Be still," he whispered so that Wheatear alone could hear him.

Then the Venerable Bead turned and raised his voice.

"I am the Venerable Bead," he said calmly.

"Greetings, Amber and Verity. There will be no violence, as I'm sure you, Amber, will comply with my request. Let Verity go, please."

Amber had not expected a peaceful approach. His nerve relaxed. His eyes darted from the Venerable Bead to the army and to Wheatear, then narrowed as he spoke. "That's not going to happen," he hissed.

"What would be the point of hurting her?" the Venerable Bead reasoned. "My army is here; at a word from me they will move in on you. Neither of us wants that, I am sure. Move away from her and no-one will be hurt."

"*HE SHOULD BE!!!*" bawled Amber, glaring furiously at Wheatear. "Look at him, thweet and cute, all shiny and polished, friendy-wendies with dear lickle Vewity, and all his super-duper fwends. Time he tasted some bad luck like the rest of us! Look at her," he said more menacingly – his eyes fixed on Wheatear, who felt like stone. "See those pwetty flowers? Know what? They're paint. Just *PAINT*."

Now Amber fixed his glittering gaze on Verity. "See the nice, metal side of this Box?" he mewed at her. "Make a lovely mirror – why not take a look?"

He thrust his big body under Verity's, forcing her

up against the Box's side – leaving her propped there, balanced and helpless.

"Awww – mirror not shiny enough to see yourself in?" His hot breath reached Verity, whose eyes were squeezed shut. "Bit rusty? How about we just try rasping you to and fro, up and down, against this nice scratchy *WALL*... and *THEN* let's see how long your painted flowers last!"

Wheatear thought of Grape, coming down here especially to scrape off his flaking paintwork on the abrasive surface.

"Put her down," said the Venerable Bead calmly. "There is something I would like to say to you." He did not move or threaten, though his dazzling oval body dwarfed Amber's.

Very slowly, Amber moved from under Verity, though he kept close contact with her. As she was lowered gradually down, Wheatear's breath was gradually expelled.

Amber fixed the Venerable Bead with his nasty yellow eyes. "This had better be good," he said.

"It is," the Venerable Bead said. "Amber, I would like you to think for a moment."

Amber rolled his eyes. "About what?" he said, as if very bored.

"About your choices," the Venerable Bead said. "You may think you have none, but that is not so. I believe you are deeply unhappy at the moment. *Non è vero?* You can change that."

Amber laughed bitterly. "Really," he spat. "I suppose you have a wando magico? You'd need one to change my chances. *Look* at me!" he shouted. "Made of foreign trash, cheap as chips, gashed by a great red idiot – oh, I'm bound to be Chosen tomorrow and live happily ever after!"

The Venerable Bead's expression did not change. "No one is trash," he said quietly, "and like me you come from a remarkable and fascinating part of the world: you from Hong Kong, I from Italy. As for your price, that is never as important as value. With your gold colouring and low cost, you could have brought pleasure to children if you had remained Outside. You chose to break away from your origins and purpose, Amber, instead of respecting them.

"As for your gash, you gave Rough no choice but to act in self-defence. Bystanders came to his assistance, so you have no proof that it was he who inflicted the blow – though it is regrettable that it happened. I aim for a peaceful environment, not a violent one. Rough had merely been trying to protect a friend from your bullying."

Wheatear's mouth fell open, and he stared at the Venerable Bead. He knew Rough? He knew about Amber and Mellow jumping on him? And he had also known who Amber was, and Lupin... What else did he know?

Amber was looking equally shocked. "I thought Rough was my mate," he said under his breath.

"He could have been," said His Excellency. "He was. But your behaviour prevented that continuing. So I am giving you the chance to change it. I can offer you an interesting and valuable life here. There are many roles for a bead who is willing to mend his ways. We can talk about what skills you have and what you would enjoy doing."

Wheatear feared he knew what both of those were. But Amber appeared to be listening. His eyes were fixed on the speaker, and he had grown still. Verity was breathing quietly, still held fast to his side. Her eyes were watching Amber's every expression.

"Are you seriously willing to do that for me?" Amber's voice was low.

"I have done the same for many others," the Venerable Bead said. "Here is your chance to prove to me that you are willing and able to accept my offer."

"I would work in your palace?" Amber asked.

"If that is the work for which you are most suited," replied the huge, shimmering bead.

"And... live there in luxury?" Amber continued.

"If you earned it," the Venerable Bead said.

Amber seemed to consider. There was a tense silence.

Then an unknown voice pierced the stillness. It seemed to come from some distance away.

"*Code T!*"

Amber's demeanour changed instantly. His evil face was wreathed in a delighted grin.

"*At last!*" he whooped. "About time! Really had you there, didn't I? Did you like my acting? Stuff your palace – I should have been on the stage! Over here, lads, past Signor Fattiano!" He pushed harder against Verity, pinning her to the Box wall.

The Venerable Bead swiftly moved aside but looked unconcerned; the army, with no command given, remained utterly immobile. Verity and Wheatear stared in confusion.

Out of the dark burst Amber's gang, heading straight towards him. Wheatear's heart plummeted. This was terrible – they were coming to Amber's rescue! He must have arranged it all in advance; 'Code T' must have been some secret signal.

And then Wheatear saw their faces. Far from triumphant, far from victorious, they were the faces of cowards, distorted with fear. Shrieking like terrified rabbits, they did not rush to aid their leader but ran straight towards the area where the solid line of army beads glinted like a steel barricade.

What was driving them to flee at such a pace?

In under a second, Wheatear had his answer. In amazement he saw, roaring behind them, two hurtling figures racing at breakneck speed. Trapped between them and the fleeing gang was someone else being forced along at the same great pace. And, as the two pursuers broke into the space, Wheatear's wood leapt like electricity.

One figure was red, and one was blue.

Immediately there came a loud, firm command.

"Surround that rabble!" the Venerable Bead

shouted, his voice carrying to each and every soldier.

Wheatear hardly knew how to turn himself quickly enough to take in the unbelievable sights before him. Amber looked stupefied, and stood like a glutinous blob. The army crisply and neatly closed in a perfect circle around his snivelling gang, and Wheatear could tell that the Venerable Bead was thanking the earless Blueberry because he was moving his mouth in a very clear way and Blueberry was watching his lips.

Most delightfully of all, the dear forms of Rough and Pebble stood, beaming but exhausted, before him.

But the names Wheatear began to speak in delight faded on his lips. As Rough gave his characteristic one-sided grin at Wheatear, the smaller bead saw that he sported another sizeable chip on his battered physique.

With deepening horror, Wheatear's gaze turned to his other dear friend. Pebble was badly wounded. The beautiful smooth surface which had first given him his name was cracked and lifted in one place; a thick flake of blue broke from him as he approached, showing that he was dull and brown beneath. But he gave a quick smile – which meant more than any words.

But what of the someone that they had been bundling along before them? Now caught up, and wedged between the familiar bodies of his friends, was another familiar figure looking equally exhausted – and certainly not beaming. Like a sickly lemon sherbet sucked thin, her face sour and shadowed, Mellow's cracked body stood, eyes darting, taking in the scene warily.

Amber was making a supreme effort to maintain his confidence. "Well how about that?" he said jauntily, leaning on Verity as if she was a useful piece of furniture. "Isn't that nice? A mate just when you need one."

The Venerable Bead did not pay any attention to Amber. "Welcome, Rough and Pebble," he said.

Wheatear opened his mouth and closed it again. He was past being surprised at anything the gigantic bead said.

"You have fulfilled your appointed task well. Thank you for finding and bringing Amber's friend. Welcome, Mellow."

Amber's and Mellow's eyes met. Wheatear watched closely. He did not trust them one dwarf beadlength.

"First, I think you have something to say to Rough," the Venerable Bead said to the unlovely pair.

"I can't think of anything," said Amber airily. "Can you, Mellow?"

Rough moved forward awkwardly.

"Look... Ah'm – Ah'm sorry that all that 'ad to 'appen, it –" he began to say.

Amber was becoming braver now with his yellow ally to support him. "He's sorry," he said sarcastically. "Well, that makes it all better, doesn't it? OK," he said in a confident tone. "We'll be reasonable – won't we, Mell? Look at us. Defaced. Damaged. Never to be Chosen. In here for life. Not nice, that. Now. I will let the little lady go," – he squeezed Verity in a fierce movement – "*if* you order your lovely helper Rough here to do a nice little bit of damage – not too much, mind, just enough – to little Pinky here. And, as Weedy Wheatear caused it all, to him too – so they can see *exactly – what – that – feels like*. I'd call that fair. Wouldn't you?"

The horror that filled Wheatear was mingled with

disbelief and pity. That a bead could even conceive of damaging another simply to stop them being Chosen – that a bead could be so bitter and filled with jealous hate that he thought this was an answer – it was so sad, so pitiful, so wasteful.

The Venerable Bead's tone became slightly sharper. "That, as you said," he intoned, "is not going to happen. In fact you have made quite an effort to deliberately hurt yourself in the past, trying to blame it on Rough here. It is quite clear to me why you chose to jump upon him. A jumping bead lands on a particular area of his own body. You were hoping to knock off the stamp you hate so much."

There was a stunned silence. Amber was completely taken aback and stood in intense embarrassment. Rough looked amazed, and it was obvious from Mellow's face that this thought had never occurred to her before. Everyone stood in shock at the Venerable Bead's blunt, candid revelation.

He spoke again. "Now, as you also said, you have a 'mate' just when you need one. So listen carefully." He spoke slowly and clearly. "I am offering you Mellow in return for Verity. If you refuse you may not see Mellow again. If you comply, you will be reunited with her. Verity for Mellow. Agreed?"

Amber tried to pull himself together. His eyes narrowed. The whole Bead Box seemed to hold its breath.

Wheatear's woodgrain tightened. Verity remained silent, squeezed by her captor against the Box wall. Wheatear wondered how long she could stand this level of fear.

Mellow's eyes were drilling into Amber's, willing him to respond.

Amber licked his treacly lips. "Agreed," he whispered huskily.

There was a slight outbreath from some beads – but no-one moved. Wheatear had never held himself so still.

The Venerable Bead said, "Verity, Mellow: exchange places."

CHAPTER II:
A GIANT LEAP

Nothing happened. The world waited.

"*Exchange places*," the Venerable Bead repeated, as if the words were underlined in heavy black ink. They seared into Wheatear's woodgrain. "Amber, you will need to release Verity, please. Keep all your movements slow."

There was a faint grating sound as Amber shifted his glinting, scarred body just enough to allow Verity to finally free herself from his constant unwanted touch. She briefly closed her eyes – then opened them and looked at Mellow, who returned her gaze. Like two cats who do not trust each other, they both began to make minute movements forward, every sound of their progress magnified by the silence, their eyes never leaving each other.

Faster, thought Wheatear frantically. *Faster – you're still too near to Amber!* But she was only doing what the Venerable Bead had told her to, he realised.

Then Wheatear's world changed. Shockingly, like a dagger being shoved through his ears from one side to another, there came a shout from very near him. His wood threatened to split.

"Code H! CODE H!"

In panic he saw the small round figure of Blueberry, still shouting the warning. He felt nothing, yet everyone was reacting in panic. So it was she who had shouted "Code T" before – and the Venerable Bead had thanked her, so it couldn't be a code of Amber's. What was Code H?

It was not long before he found out. Above him a horribly familiar sound was growing ever louder. A magnified thrum – no, hugely magnified: a mumbling, chumbling and roaring...

"The Hand is upon us!" the Venerable Bead

thundered. "Make for the side, instantly! Those already touching it, stay!"

Wheatear's thoughts whirled. How could this be happening? But at least this time he knew what to do. He no longer cared if he was Chosen – in fact, at this moment, it would be disaster. He cared only for Verity's safety, and his only desire was to be with her.

His thoughts seemed to organise themselves at lightning speed. Amber, Verity, Mellow, Pebble, and Rough all knew the trick of making for the side even before the Venerable Bead had commanded them to go there. He tried to get inside each of their minds. The last thing Amber would want would be for Verity to be Chosen. He hated her prettiness and wanted to spoil her chances – so he would push her to the side and hold her there.

But Amber was already pushing Verity to the side, Wheatear reasoned. He had been holding her there all this time, in front of them all. Everyone knew where he was. If he stayed there, the Venerable Bead would stay with him. No: Wheatear knew what Amber would do. He would see the Hand as the answer to his prayers – if he ever prayed at all. He would take advantage of the awful confusion and make off with Verity to another part of the side, probably an area the others would least expect. He might even try to cross the whole base of the Box, where the Hand rarely if ever reached.

And where Amber went, Mellow would go.

Pebble and Rough would certainly not leave Mellow, who they had been told to find, bring, and guard. Wheatear also felt – and hoped – that they would not leave *him*. And the Venerable Bead, he was sure, would not desert any of them.

So all of them would head for where Amber was heading – and Wheatear would have to do the same.

Thanks to Blueberry's sensory gift, the beads had been given enough warning time to react. Wheatear, whose thoughts had taken only a split second, could see Amber and Mellow trundling along in the gloom ahead. In front of them they were carelessly buffeting and bowling the small, vulnerable figure of Verity. Where Pebble, Rough and the Venerable Bead were, he did not know, and beads were pushing past him in every direction. Meanwhile the well-remembered cries of fear came echoing down from the many layers above him, where presumably the Hand was now reaching, searching and rooting.

He could not lose sight of Amber!

By now, Amber's gang, seeing their last possible chance of freedom, had surged toward the middle of the Box, desperate to escape the Venerable Bead – and possibly in the faint hope of being Chosen. But they had not reckoned on the Venerable Bead's expertise. He had seen it all before. Spotting their plan, he had ordered his army to pursue them, and now the silver snake was moving in on their feeble, screaming forms.

Terror-stricken, uncouth and lumbering, their panic made them easy bait for the cool metallic army. Soon the gang had given up any attempt at struggling. They knew that, if they showed violence, the army beads could be instantly instructed to fracture them into mere splinters – and, after a few minutes, all that might remain of them were small, isolated circular heaps of finely ground dust.

Wheatear turned away. They were not his concern, nor his priority.

For a ghastly instant he thought he had lost sight of Amber – but, staring into the murky Deeps, he saw the ill-matched trio still stumbling ahead. It seemed that, as he had thought, Amber was heading right across the bottom of the box. Wheatear wondered if, even now, Amber might still be trying to scrape the stamp off his derrière.

As this unpleasant thought entered his wood, he was astonished to see Grape. The scabrous purple bead sat happily on the base of the Box, laughing out loud as hundreds of beads knocked into him and raced past him. Lumps of dry purple paint were breaking off him and littering the floor. Beneath, Wheatear saw that Grape was silky and silvery grey. Grape was jigging about and whooping, "Fantastic! Yeah – hit me! Fantastic!"

Wheatear wondered how much more bizarre his new life could possibly grow. Then he remembered: Grape had known exactly where the Venerable Bead's palace was. He must have a good sense of direction.

"Grape!" he yelled. "Where are we?"

"In the middle, matey," beamed Grape, "where I can get the most traffic!"

Wheatear managed to gasp his thanks, and then looked ahead. There was no sign of Amber. In the brief time Wheatear had been distracted by Grape, Amber had disappeared.

Desperately, Wheatear turned back to the purple

bead who was now an almost perfect pearly grey. Above and around them the turmoil continued.

"Did you see a big chap – treacly, amber-coloured?" Wheatear asked.

"Sure," Grape said, before thanking a cube-shaped bead for barging into him to send another flake of violet paint ricocheting into the hot air. "Really seemed interested in how I was getting my paint knocked off – almost as if he wanted it for himself – except he wasn't painted, and seemed in a hurry, so I –"

"*Where did he go?*" squealed Wheatear.

"That way – to the side, I guess," Grape said, nodding in an unexpected direction. "Had two others with him: stripey ugly girl, and a gorgeous little –"

"Thanks," Wheatear panted, and headed determinedly where Grape had indicated.

His thoughts raced. So Amber had deliberately tried to throw him off the scent. Into the middle, then off to the side at an angle. Well, Wheatear had to admire his strategy. And no wonder he was interested in how Grape's paint was being knocked off – one knock like that and he might be rid of the stamp on his...

But Wheatear had no time to dwell on that now.

Never had he moved so fast. He rolled, bounced, and leapt along in any way he could. He briefly wondered if the triplets would be impressed if they could see him, but banished the thought from his mind. He could not think of his friends now.

With a sudden jolt, he stopped. He must have been moving more quickly than even he had realised. For in front of him, not a great distance away, was the wall of the Box – and against the wall stood Amber.

The hefty toffee-coloured bead and the small brown one faced each other, in earshot of each other's panting breaths. There was now little other sound apart from the thrum, and the muted sound of beads moaning in the layers above them. It was clear that the Hand had finished its search.

Then Amber's mouth began to expand horribly in a stretched, wide grin.

"Here we are," he said softly. "Nice and safe at the nice, safe side."

Wheatear looked him full in the eye. "Where is she?" he asked quietly.

"She?" Amber enquired. "She? Oh, of course," he laughed lightly, "you mean my lovely friend Mellow. Kind of you to ask after her, show concern."

Wheatear was thinking rapidly. Where was Verity? Where were the others? But he could not rely on them; they could be anywhere in the Bead Box.

At this point, Wheatear thought he heard a slight noise to the right of Amber. He put it down to the ringing in his ears and his sharpened state of mind, but a second later he heard it again – a limping, trailing, scraping noise, always getting nearer.

Wheatear paused. Something about it seemed familiar...

Then he knew.

Sidling in, with a chilling grin to match Amber's own, came Mellow. Her cracked yellow body pushed a small, flowered bead unwillingly along the wall until the painted petals touched the faceted surface of her evil partner. The sinister limping ceased.

The two bullies leaned in on the delicate pink bead between them, exerting increasing pressure. They reminded Wheatear of a pair of jewellery pliers squeezing together on the fastening of a necklace.

Amber put his face very close to Verity's. "Like a little squeeze, do yer?" he breathed.

Wheatear's wood turned hot.

Pale with fear, Verity flashed a desperate look at Wheatear and her dry mouth opened. She seemed about to speak. Instantly Amber thrust his face into hers.

"*SHUT. UP.*" He bawled as loudly as he could into her terrified eyes.

Wheatear was filled with some feeling he could not place. His brain seemed to be expanding. "Move away from her, both of you," he heard himself say.

"Ooooh, me fwightened," said Amber. "Better do as he says, hadn't we, Mell?" He pretended to shake with fear.

Mellow's eyes met Amber's, and she smirked. A look seemed to pass between them. "Yes, let's move away from her," Mellow cooed sweetly.

Momentarily, Wheatear was thrown by this. Surely they weren't actually doing as he wanted? No – he knew them too well. There would be some plan. But what?

What happened next took only seconds, but

would be in Wheatear's memory for ever. The two evil beads began slowly to move away from Verity, each backing off a short distance away on either side of her, leaving her stranded in the space between them and still against the side of the Box. Wheatear's attention was torn from Verity to the evil lemon face and triumphant cackling laugh of the crouching Mellow – and in horror he suddenly understood their plan. On one side Mellow was now leaning back to launch all her green-streaked weight at her trapped and defenceless victim; on the other Amber also pulled back, ready to take a leap inwards and fling his much greater bulk against Verity's tender wood.

A voice came clearly and strongly to the front of Wheatear's mind. He recognised it as the Venerable Bead's – and, though the giant bead was not present, it was as if his voice was so close it was within Wheatear himself. It was speaking words – words that Wheatear had heard before. Words that seemed underlined in black...

With crystal clarity, he heard in his heated brain the Venerable Bead's command:

"*Exchange places...*"

At once the expanding feeling in his brain seemed

to reach bursting point. He could not have explained what the feeling was. All he knew was that it made him feel strong, and came out in a huge call to Verity. With all the power in his lungs, he yelled:

"*TO ME!*"

He prayed she would understand, and dare to obey him.

She did.

Gathering all her remaining strength, and placing all her faith in him, Verity dashed forward towards Wheatear. And as she did so, the pressured sensation in Wheatear burst free, and he seemed powered with the most glorious energy and confidence. With all his wooden might, Wheatear hurled himself over Verity's head, flying as if unseen wings had sprouted from his grain to support him. Gazing downwards as he sailed, he saw the upturned faces of numerous beads staring at him from below – among them, to his amazement, Rough, Pebble and the Venerable Bead. And his young life seemed to play like a slow motion film before him. His necklace, his time in the charity shop, the wait behind the cabinet, his arrival in the Bead Box, his friends, Verity. *Verity...*

With a snap his body landed where hers had been

against the side of the Box. And the moment when he exchanged places with Verity was the moment when Amber and Mellow, crazed with resentment and revenge, were flinging themselves inwards with their entire and combined force on either side of what they had thought would be Verity's body, intent on a massive and devastating collision.

Wheatear knew his moment had come. But death did not seem so bad. Verity would live, and she would be among friends. He steeled himself for the double-sided blow.

It came.

His world went pure white and he had no hearing. It was rather wonderful: a world of silence and brilliant light.

A world that only lasted a beadbreath.

For, then, sound came crashing in, and it seemed the sound of a thousand indrawn gasps.

After a few seconds, Wheatear's eyes – which he found were screwed tight – dared to unlock.

He looked downwards at his body – then inspected it more closely.

It was unharmed.

He lifted his eyes and saw in front of him the wall

of the Box, where he had landed in Verity's place.

Slowly he allowed his gaze to drift to his right. Beside him the body of Mellow – with a slow, ripping sound – gradually split down the line of her earlier wound and fell apart. Seconds later she lay bisected, like the yellow-rinded fruit after which she was named, rocking in two uneven pieces.

Wresting his eyes from the sight, and with a horrible foreboding, Wheatear turned to his left.

Amber gave Wheatear one last look of dreadful knowledge before his body reeled towards the wall, leaned forwards, and collapsed head down into slithering lumps like a windscreen smacked by a rock. The last Wheatear saw of his enemy was a spreading stamp spelling the words 'Hong Kong', before the wretched bead was reduced to a spoonful of powdered plastic.

In their weakened states their fates had been sealed: Amber from his scar, years of shuffling shame and grinding himself away; Mellow from the deep fissure she had sustained from the attack on Rough.

There was a sound like a tyre gradually deflating. Wheatear realised it was the slow release of breath from all the beads around him.

Sickened, Wheatear could only turn from the gritty remains. His own horror was unimportant. He cared only for the safety of Verity, who was silently shivering. The Venerable Bead must have given orders to his army, for Wheatear realised that Verity was protected by a solid circle of army beads. He approached her and the soldiers parted, allowing him to her side. There Wheatear gently leant his head against hers. They stood very still, eyes resting, breathing together, without a word.

"Wheatear," came a deep, gentle voice. "Wheatear."

Wearily, the small brown bead lifted his head and looked into the iridescent face of the Venerable Bead. Turning politely, he and Verity stood before the glorious figure to whom they would both be grateful for ever.

The Venerable Bead spoke to a couple of soldiers

in the protective circle. "You two take this lady to the dwarf beads of the bedchamber. Show her every care."

The soldiers moved to Verity's right and left respectfully. Wheatear watched as, with surprising gentleness, they led her carefully to the main palace door to be attended by their leader's personal servants.

To the rest of his soldiers, the Venerable Bead called, "At ease." Then, turning, he said, "Come, Wheatear."

An eerie silence settled on the area. The contrast after the din of the Hand's visit was stunning, though that seemed a lifetime away.

Wheatear turned slowly and surveyed the ghastly scene. A dry taste was in his mouth; his eyes and body were dusted with the dead. A sick despair filled him, but he stretched his body a little to ease it from its rigid state. *Perhaps now,* he thought, *all shall be well. Perhaps now, at last, I can simply be with my friends again.*

He sighed heavily. He had no wish to stay among the grim remains. He turned wearily to the palace.

Then he froze.

From behind him, where the bodies of his two

enemies lay, there came a low moan. Hardly daring to turn his body, Wheatear allowed his eyes to pull him round little by little until he stared towards the side of the Box where the two halves of Mellow's body lay immobile.

Infinitesimally, one of the pieces moved.

Wheatear felt all moisture leave his wood. A small involuntary noise escaped his lips.

The larger portion of Mellow's body was rocking; it seemed to be trying to right itself like a turtle balanced on its shell.

Wheatear dashed forward. Leaning his weight on one side of Mellow's raw interior, he flipped it over with enormous effort.

On the other side was Mellow's face. Her eyes were glazed. A hideous gurgling came from her drooling mouth.

Wheatear never knew what made him shout what he did. His Excellency was only a few beadrolls away; the army beads were in the palace and would have been there in an instant. But he was so tired, so tired. And he was frightened, young, and lonely. He needed the comfort of those he loved most.

"Rough!" he shouted, weeping. "Pebble! Rough!"

A little way off, a large red figure struggled forward from the direction of the palace. Behind it, Wheatear made out a familiar colour – a pigeon blue-grey, unlike any other bead he knew.

Wheatear stood aside and indicated what remained of Mellow.

It was then that the Venerable Bead appeared and, without a word, led the exhausted brown bead into his palace.

CHAPTER 12:
WHEATEAR QUERCUS

For most of the next day, Wheatear slept. He drifted in and out of a dreamlike daze, sometimes able to focus on the unknown space where he lay, and at others twitching in a world in his mind where Amber lurked and Hands swirled and beads broke into horrible halves in front of him.

But always, when he woke, he found comforting beads around him, and the following day he felt rested, strong and well.

He realised he had been carried to a peaceful room completely composed of white beads, and was lying on a white beaded bed. During the late afternoon, the chief servant, who had first led Wheatear into the palace, waddled up to his bedside. After informing him that this was the palace infirmary, he delivered a message from His Excellency: Verity was fully recovered, and if Wheatear was also well there would be a celebration in their honour in the throne room that evening.

Wheatear was full to the brim with questions. Where was Verity? Where was Mellow? What had happened to Pebble and Rough? But the servant's only reply was, "I am not at liberty to say, sir. His Excellency will explain all this evening."

Wheatear wanted to race to the throne room at once, but the calmly efficient nurse beads made it clear that he should continue to rest.

He must have fallen asleep, for he woke later to find one of them gently nudging him and saying it was time to go.

He found his wood had been carefully polished, though scratches remained. The chief steward appeared once more. The beaded infirmary doors clicked neatly shut behind him and he was again led into the vaulted, opulent main chamber, which was crammed with ranks of expectant beads.

Resplendent upon his shimmering throne sat the

Venerable Bead, appearing more radiant than ever. He smiled at Wheatear, but instead of greeting him spoke words which made the brown bead's heart leap in joy.

"Bring in the little lady," he commanded. "She has waited long enough."

Wheatear jumped as, with a swift zipping sound, a pile of beads divided crisply into two walls to reveal an arched grotto. There was a moment's wait, and then a dwarf bead entered leading in the small unharmed figure of Verity, as pink and petalled as before. Wheatear thought she looked as beautiful as it was possible for anything to look.

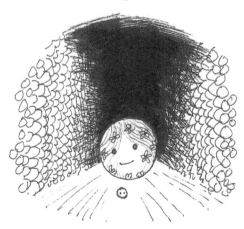

The moment they stood together, the crowd erupted into ear-splitting cheers. Wheatear heard his name chanted over and over, and to his astonishment he was hoisted high on the heads of larger beads – among them Pebble and Rough. He was carried along under the kaleidoscopic roof, the dwarf beads constantly changing their patterns in his honour, while others bounced on the lavishly decorative floor of the palace in bead applause.

Wheatear glimpsed Blueberry joyfully dancing around, enjoying the huge rhythmic sensation. From his throne the Venerable Bead laughed with pleasure – and below, Verity simply beamed.

Finally the noise abated, and the beads lowered Wheatear, somewhat to his relief, on to a miniature footstool. Verity sat on a similar one beside him. Facing His Excellency, they were surrounded by the throng of well-wishers who, although virtual strangers, stood smiling proudly.

Bursting with pride, Wheatear formally introduced Verity to his friends. She exchanged a warm smile with Pebble, and said it didn't matter at all when poor Rough babbled an apology for his battered condition in front of a lady. "Considering how much you have done to help us, dear Rough," she said, "I think your appearance is the very last thing that matters." Then she reached to his great craggy face and gently kissed him.

It may have been the effect of the palace's rose-tinted light upon Rough's countenance, but it certainly seemed to Wheatear that his large, red face grew suddenly redder, and he mumbled something while shuffling awkwardly about. Wheatear giggled.

"And you, Pebble," said Verity, turning to the wounded blue bead earnestly. "It was through talking about you that I became such friends with Wheatear. I am indebted to you for all you have done."

Pebble inclined towards her. "It was a pleasure, ma'am," he said gravely.

"*Molto bene. Molto bene*," the Venerable Bead said. "That is enough for the moment. Wheatear, Verity: it is so good – *so* good – to have you with us. And now I know that you have many questions to ask. The time has come for them to be answered. And for that, I think you are entitled to some privacy. Chief steward."

The small, distorted glass bead strutted forward and signalled to the assembly to depart from the chamber. Servants, guests, entertainers and nurses filed from the throne room, smiling and nodding at Wheatear as they left. The soldiers followed, upright and expressionless as ever – though some pairs of eyes sneaked him an encouraging look.

Although touched by their support, Wheatear was greatly relieved not to have to share his questions with all of them – and grateful to the Venerable Bead for his understanding. With the chamber quiet, Wheatear opened his mouth to begin – but his host was speaking once more.

"However," the Venerable Bead said, "before you commence, there are others whose presence I think you will mind less." With his huge side he tapped on his throne, and the beaded portals snapped open once again.

Tumbling into the chamber, and squeaking wildly, bobbed the small, rosy bodies of Pippin, Robin and Cherry. Behind them, Bee's spotted form zigzagged to and fro. More sedately, but with an eager gait, proceeded the deep and glowing figures of Velvet and Lupin. Rough and Pebble moved quickly forward to join them. Wheatear leapt from his seat and bumped and bounced against each of them in joyous greeting; jumping from her little footstool, Verity laughed with pure delight.

Then what a mixture of emotions poured out among the reunited beads! Tears, laughter, questions and news passed non-stop between them, though they overlapped so much that hardly any could be heard. It was clear that the Hand had found none of them. They had pressed themselves to the side, the dwarf beads had located them, and the army had been sent to escort them safely here.

Eventually things quietened down. All eleven beads sat comfortably in a circle, which included the throne, and in front of the mighty Venerable Bead even the triplets sat in silence and respect.

"Now, Wheatear," the Venerable Bead said warmly.

Wheatear had so many questions that they came out in no particular sequence or order, and his friends threw in further reminders when needed. Gradually they pieced together what had happened. The 'reliable source' from whom the dwarf beads had heard of Verity's whereabouts was Rough himself, who had been known to the Venerable Bead for many years.

"Saved me, 'e did," said Rough simply. "I 'it rock bottom – huh, literally, the Deeps – when I first took a real look at meself an' realised I'd never be Chosen again. I wasn't behavin' well, if you know what I mean. This wonderful gentleman fahnd me, listened to me, believed in me, and said I 'ad skills 'e could use."

At this point a polite cough came from a lofty height. Lupin did not need to lie down in the Deeps, as there was nowhere to fall to.

"If you will excuse me interjecting, Your Excellency," dropped his sonorous tones from above, "perhaps I may take this opportunity to at last thank you personally for doing something very similar for me. This is the first chance I have had to express my sincere gratitude."

"It is a pleasure to have been of assistance," the Venerable Bead acknowledged.

After a suitable pause, Rough continued his explanation. The job entrusted to him was to 'keep an eye' on things in the Upper Middle layer – helped by the network of dwarf beads known as the beadvine, who could pass messages along rapidly to any part of the Box while remaining largely unseen. Rough had recommended Pebble to His Excellency as another dependable helper. Later, news had reached the Venerable Bead of Amber's cruel tendencies towards a newcomer.

"Amber thought he was getting in with Rough, little knowing Rough was posted to watch him," explained Pebble. "And I –"

He stopped.

"You were posted to watch me," Wheatear finished. Yet another thing for which he would be eternally grateful to the Venerable Bead.

"When I left yer, it was to report back to 'is Excellency," said Rough. "I said I could do that through the beadvine, but Pebble said 'is orders were to leave you alone to learn for yourself."

"*Maniere forti* – tough love," the Venerable Bead said quietly. "I know Pebble found my orders very hard."

So it was the Venerable Bead who had asked Pebble to let Wheatear fend for himself. Wheatear thought about how lonely and frightened he had been when Pebble and Rough had left him. Yet it had led to him finding his own bravery. In the long term, it was a wise decision. It had made him who he was. Good things came out of bad things.

The next task which His Excellency had given them was to isolate Amber by removing and guarding Mellow and the gang, as he knew Amber would be weaker without them.

"That's why we were away so long," Pebble explained. "We had to keep Mellow away from the Deeps. The beadvine kept us informed and we knew Amber and Verity were down there."

"I thought you were lost after the Hand's first visit," Wheatear said.

"Cor, me an' Peb was so worried abaht you, you got no idea," Rough said with feeling. "We realised you wouldn't know that trick, pressin' against the side. We cursed ourselves for forgettin' ter tell yer! Nearly broke our 'earts when we found you'd gorn."

"But you'd gone too," Wheatear said. "I thought you might even have been –"

"Chosen?" Rough said, and smiled ruefully. "Lookin' like this? I don't think so!"

"Of course, I was made aware of the cause of this, and the earlier attack on Rough," the Venerable Bead commented, shifting slightly on his throne.

"By the dwarf beads?" Robin asked.

"Partly," His Excellency said, "but they were not responsible for reporting the initial incidents. Blueberry saw to that!"

"So she can detect any unusual disturbance in the entire Box," Lupin marvelled. "What remarkable sensitivity. A gift indeed."

"I understand that Code H must mean the Hand," said Wheatear, "but what was Code T?"

"Turbulence," the Venerable Bead said. "A useful term for any eventuality. Otherwise we'd have to have Code F for Fracas, Code S for Skirmish –"

"Code O for Ouch," giggled Pippin.

Everyone laughed, glad of the momentary relief from serious matters.

"So – what happened to you both?" Verity asked Pebble and Rough, looking sadly at their most recent wounds.

Pebble explained: "We told Amber's gang quite truthfully that he needed to be alone for a certain task to be accomplished, and didn't want them hurt – and that Rough would protect them and keep them away from the Deeps for their own safety. Mellow is frightened of Rough, and thought she'd be safer with the gang around her. She went along with it."

But once this had happened, things had taken an ugly turn. Burning with resentment that their jump on Rough had failed, and that she had been wounded thanks to him, Mellow thought she'd try again with the gang around her. That night, Mellow had commanded them to launch a full-scale attack on Rough and Pebble. She wanted to get her own back on Rough – and hoped to ruin Pebble's chances of being Chosen.

But she had not reckoned on the cowardice of the gang, the undiminished strength of Rough, or the determination of Pebble to stand up for what was right. They had fought bravely, again supported by beads who had seen what was going on – leaving the gang howling and rolling off to escape their blows. It had then been an easy matter to keep Mellow with them.

This left an uncomfortable question hanging in the air – but it had to be asked.

"Vhat now is happening to them – this gang and the Mellow?" Velvet asked worriedly.

"The last time I saw the gang they were heading to the middle," Wheatear recalled, "with the soldiers after them."

The ten friends heard that some of the gang had been taken by the Hand. Wheatear was rather surprised by this – as most were, frankly, not the kind of beads he had imagined would be Chosen. The Venerable Bead explained that the Hand did not always simply Choose; it Tidied too. Beads that were considered completely unusable would probably be fed to the Lung – and their fighting had left a number in an unusable state.

As for the rest, the well-trained army had rounded them up with no difficulty. They had been brought to the palace for training.

"Training? As what?" Bee asked.

"The choice is theirs," the Venerable Bead said. "Perhaps firstly as assistants – and possibly, if they develop these skills well, as helpers to those in distress in the Deeps. They are used to doing another's bidding, but they need to learn that there are good, helpful and valuable tasks to be done – and by doing them, satisfaction and reward can be gained.

"As we saw with Amber, I can offer – but it is up to the beads themselves whether they accept or refuse. My feeling is that most of this gang will actually be relieved to be away from Amber's evil influence, and be content to become law-abiding. They only served him through fear, and I believe they will be glad to have a bit of peace."

"What horrors one bully can cause," Lupin said solemnly. Everyone was silent.

"And Mellow?" Pebble asked eventually.

"Mellow had an extraordinary escape," the Venerable Bead remarked. "I have visited her several times in the infirmary, and we have spoken together at length. I have offered her a role here in the palace, and – unlike Amber – I find her to have a strong desire to mend her ways. Everyone – *everyone*," he emphasised, seeing the looks of incredulity on some of the faces before him, "should be given a second chance."

"Like I was," Rough said under his breath.

"And I," Lupin added quietly.

"Mellow has told me a lot about her past," the Venerable Bead continued. "She has been a deeply unhappy bead, and a victim of circumstance. She knew she was disliked, and didn't know how to change that. Mellow knows she got involved with the wrong set and accepts that the way she behaved was very wrong.

"*Bene, bene* – she is certainly better off without Amber. I believe if I find the right beads to work with her patiently, she will find fulfilment and be a capable helper. She has asked me, without me suggesting it, to apologise to all concerned."

There was silence as all the beads took this in. Wheatear found that he felt very sorry for Mellow. Anyone can be a victim of circumstance, after all. And anyone can change if they are given the chance.

His Excellency spoke again.

"We shall never know the identity of the bead who actually caused the split in Mellow's wood," he said, "but whoever it was managed it in such a way that her face and ears are undamaged. True, she has lost a portion of her back –"

"Will it be fed to the Lung?" Wheatear asked in horror.

"The Lung only removes unusable things," the Venerable Bead replied. "Mellow's back is strong, striped and curved. She is happy for it to be used as a rocker for small, young beads."

I know three little red ones who'd enjoy that, thought Wheatear. The triplets were already exchanging excited glances.

"In the infirmary," the Venerable Bead continued firmly.

The triplets hastily rearranged their faces.

Then a single word from the Venerable Bead dropped into the stillness.

"Amber..."

Wheatear seemed to see a heavy lump of molten toffee falling into cold water.

"Amber," His Excellency continued, "or rather Amber's remains, are at this moment being removed by the army."

He must have seen the bewildered expressions on the faces of the younger beads, for he went on, "It is a job with which my army is familiar. The dust of dead beads discourages the Hand from visiting – which, although disruptive, is essential if any beads are to be Chosen. The dust also dirties our environment and is distressing to other beads.

"The soldiers' method is perhaps unusual, but efficacious. They scoop up the finest dust in their ears – and, when full, line themselves up one atop the other all the way up to the Crack with their ears perfectly aligned. My larger and stronger servants then blow upwards into the ear of the lowest soldier, and the dust will be disgorged over the top of the Box, to be removed by the Lung. The whole operation is, as I say, very efficient – though of course during the procedure the soldiers cannot hear a word, so to give them any command is useless."

"In one ear and out the other," Lupin commented; then added hastily, "oh... if you'll pardon the rather unfortunate expression."

There was a tense silence – and then the triplets snorted, and everyone burst into laughter.

Wheatear looked around him, remembering how he had viewed the Deeps when he first heard about them. If someone had told him that in a few weeks' time he would be rolling around in mirth with ten good friends, he would simply not have believed them. Even the Lung had proved to be a useful piece of equipment – he expected Grape's discarded paintwork would be fed to it in due course. It was strange how good things came out of bad things...

When the laughter had subsided and the beads had settled into a thoughtful silence again, it was Verity's small, clear voice which spoke.

"What were they going to do to me?" she asked.

Everyone turned to look at her anxiously.

"It's all right," Verity said. "I want to know."

The Venerable Bead leaned back on his massive throne and cleared his throat.

"Having spoken to Mellow," he said, addressing Verity directly, "I am inclined to believe it was never her intention or Amber's to end your life or theirs. They were bitter – and jealous of your beauty, instead of looking at it with pleasure and delight. They knew you were painted, and had seen how some beads lose their paintwork – Pebble, Grape, to name but two. And they wanted to rob you of your flowers – to damage your chances of being Chosen, but mostly to hurt Wheatear."

Everyone was quiet again. In that second, Wheatear remembered the conversation with Grape. Amber had not been interested in getting someone to knock his Hong Kong stamp off. He had been interested in how easy it was to knock paint off. Paint like Verity's unique, delicate, beautiful, lovingly hand-painted flowers.

Hand-painted, thought Wheatear. He pondered on how differently hands could behave. If human hands went around destroying and damaging real flowers because they were so beautiful, what would be the gain? It made no sense.

"Have you any other questions, Wheatear?" the Venerable Bead asked, turning in his direction.

"Yes," he replied, coming back from his musings. He turned to Pebble and Rough. "How did you find me? When the Hand came, we lost each other. I knew you'd make for the side, but – how did you know exactly which part I'd be in?"

Pebble half laughed at the memory. "Ironically, we have Amber to thank for that," he said.

"Yeah," Rough agreed, "cor blimey. Never 'eard

anyone shaht 'Shut up' so loud. That'd blast the dust out of yer ears, orright. We just headed straight for where it came from. 'Elped us no end."

Yet again, thought Wheatear, remembering the horror of Amber bawling his cruel words into Verity's face. Yet again, good things out of bad things.

"And if that hadn't been enough, we'd have still found you," Pebble added, "because the next shout came from you, Wheatear."

"*To meeeeeee!!!*" imitated everybody, cheering at the memory.

"That was some leap," Bee said in undisguised admiration.

"Too right," said Cherry, while Pippin hurled himself off his footstool, mouth wide open, yelling "*To meeee!*" again.

"I know it sounded silly," Wheatear said, "but I had to think of a quick way to make Verity understand. I knew if I said the phrase that was in my mind, she wouldn't come."

"What was the phrase in your mind?" Verity asked.

"Exchange places," Wheatear said.

The beads all looked at him.

"The phrase I used to request Mellow and Verity to do the same," the Venerable Bead said pensively, almost to himself. "Well – one never knows when something one says may be useful to others."

Verity too was thoughtful.

"You're right," she said. "If you had asked me to exchange places, I wouldn't have done – because –"

"– it would have put Wheatear in danger," Pebble finished. "By saying 'To me,' he made you think he just wanted you to join him."

"It didn't sound silly at all," Verity said. "And it probably saved my life."

"Vell done, Veetear," Velvet said, impressed. "I am very undistressed. I am feeling I vill make the singing!"

"Well done indeed," the Venerable Bead said. "And now, I think you have one more question to ask. Am I right?"

The small brown bead marvelled once again. How did this weighty antique bead who lived his life in the Deeps know so very, very much?

"Speak, Wheatear," His Excellency commanded. "It is the question everyone wants to know, but it should be you who asks it."

Wheatear looked around at his friends. Their faces were serious and waiting. He drew breath.

"My question is..." He began hesitantly, for he did not like to remember it. "My question is – when Amber and M-mellow jumped in on me – how come I survived?"

The enormous, intricate bead looked down to the plain brown one.

"I was there when you shouted to Verity," said the Venerable Bead. "How come I didn't stop you?"

The little bead had not thought of this. One command to the soldiers and they could have barred his way, or surrounded him. He could not answer.

The Venerable Bead appeared to change the subject. "Verity, come forward," he said – and although His Excellency's multi-hued body was dazzling, Wheatear thought the pink petalled bead was the most beautiful in the room.

Little Verity stood at the throne of the Venerable

Bead and lifted her tiny face to his giant one.

"Thank you, Your Excellency," she said simply, "for not stopping him."

"Thank *you*, dearest Verity," the Venerable Bead replied.

Verity smiled in surprise.

"Me? Why?" she asked, forgetting to be formal in her curiosity.

"Because it is through you, *piccolina*, that I have gained so much joy," the Venerable Bead said, and his voice seemed tinged with a humble sadness. "Over the years, as I have sat down here, I have watched beads come and go – beads governed by hate, rejected because of some disfigurement, eaten away by jealousy... Yes: it can be a sordid layer, the Deeps. But you and your friends have brought a freshness – a purity. Almost..."

He paused.

"...almost like being Outside again," he finished gently.

"Sit by me, you two young ones," he went on in his old, deep voice.

Wheatear and Verity obediently moved, one to each side of his bead-encrusted throne.

"Your names are wisely chosen," he said softly, "for you, Verity, will always represent truth. And Wheatear," he said, turning to the small brown bead who looked up at him. "Who gave you your name?"

"Pebble did, Your Excellency," Wheatear replied.

"Its choice shows wisdom," the Venerable Bead said, "for though an ear of wheat may be small, it has the power of growth. And now I have another question. What name did I call you when you first visited the palace?"

Wheatear frowned. What had this to do with anything?

He organised his thoughts. "Acorn, Your Excellency," he said, remembering his slight indignation.

"Acorn," the great fatherly bead smiled. "It must have been instinctive. You are growing, not in size, but into something strong and worthwhile and valuable. Great oaks, as you said..."

"But, Your Excellency," Wheatear said, overawed by the honour of these words, "I am not really an ear of wheat, or an acorn. I am only a little lump of wood."

"But what wood are you, Wheatear?" the Venerable Bead asked, looking down at him.

Wheatear's eyes met those of the gigantic bead, set in their kaleidoscopic surface. "I don't know," he whispered.

"*Quercia*. You are oak, Wheatear," the Venerable Bead said gently. "Wheatear Quercus. One of the strongest materials in the whole world."

"But..." The small bead looked at the matching one beside him. "But that means..."

"That's right," the great bead said. "Verity is oak too. They would never have managed to kill her. Now, go into the world and grow."

EPILOGUE:
THE THREAD IS TIED

"It'll be a *really* beautiful necklace, won't it?" the girl asked, her hair hanging over the sides of her face.

"As beautiful as we can make it," the older woman said, sifting the many beads in her hand as she spoke. "Now that you're grown-up enough to look after it," she added with a smile.

"Did I really have such a temper?" The girl looked up, her eyes alight with amusement and fascination. "*Did* I, really? Stamping and screaming and breaking it into pieces?"

"You did. Don't you remember? I was very cross and said you weren't allowed any jewellery again if that's what you were going to do with it."

"Until I was more sensible," the girl said. "Which I am now."

Suddenly she gave an excited gasp.

"Ooh look! Stop – that one in your hand."

A small pink bead painted with tiny white flowers had appeared in the assortment the woman held.

"Oh, I must have that one!" said the girl in ecstasy. "It's *sooooo* lovely – let's have it in the middle."

"That was from my bracelet when I was little!" the woman said. "I loved it, but all the others lost their paint. All right – so now we need something to go round it."

"Something plain," the girl said firmly. "To help that pretty one stand out specially."

They filled their hands with the rattling mountains of beads and let them trickle back into the box, their eyes sharp as they searched.

"There's this one," the woman said, holding out a small wooden bead that was dark brown in colour. "It's from that necklace I got at the charity shop. The one you broke! I think all the others got lost."

"Sorry..." said the girl, grimacing. "But you always say good things come out of bad things. It's a bit scratched, but it's just the same size and type as the pink one. We need another one the same though, to match it on the other side."

They searched again. There were minute glass beads at the very bottom of the box that got under their nails.

"There isn't another one," the girl sighed finally.

"What about this?" the woman asked. In her hand lay a dull blue bead against her wedding ring. "I remember the necklace this came from," she added softly.

"That won't do!" the girl said in surprise. "It doesn't match."

"No, but look..." The woman lifted the blue with her fingernail. "It's like a shell of plaster – it comes off. It's old."

"How old? Was it yours?"

"Oh, ages ago," said the woman. "Another life," she murmured.

"What?"

"Pardon," corrected the woman. "Erm, another life – for the bead, I mean. Look: it's solid wood underneath, and the same size – just like this other one."

"We could make it match, you mean?"

"We could make it new," the woman said. "We could clean up this blue one and then rub them both with beeswax, and then they would both be dark brown and glossy. They'd match perfectly."

"And then they could go on either side of the flowery one and smell like honey!" the girl rejoiced. She arranged the three beads in the palm of her hand, in order. "They're like a story," she said. "Beginning, middle and end."

"And they'll have a thread," the woman said. "Like a story." She picked up a smooth narrow cord and snipped a length with small fine scissors.

"What do you mean?"

"All stories need a thread. In fact old stories were often *about* thread – spinning, weaving, stitching..."

"Like Sleeping Beauty!" the girl exclaimed. "And Rumpelstiltskin, weaving straw into gold..."

"Yes – and there are lots more. Women used to tell them as they spun their wool or sewed their seams, because stories are always about what you know, and that's what they did all day. You've heard people saying 'spinning a yarn' or 'weaving a tale' or 'following the thread of a story'? So – all good stories have a thread."

"Like my beads," the girl said. "Their story will have a thread."

She stopped and looked up.

"I wonder what their story is."

"I wonder," the woman said, almost to herself.

The girl studied the three small spheres, suddenly quiet. "Poor beads," she said gently. "It must be sad, leaving all their friends back in the bead box."

"Oh, I'm sure they'll be more than happy on a necklace."

"More than happy? Really?" asked the girl.

"Truly," said her mother.

QUESTIONS FOR BOOK CLUBS

<u>Prologue</u>
1. Can you think of any examples in history, or your own life, where good things came out of bad things? How can we make this happen?
2. What makes bullies want to bully?

<u>Chapter 1</u>
1. Are there similarities between the Bead Box and human society?
2. Mellow and Amber hide things about themselves. Why do people do this? Are there good and bad reasons to hide the truth?

<u>Chapter 2</u>
1. Why is it important that we have names?
2. What do you think of Wheatear's personality?

<u>Chapter 3</u>
1. What do you think is the story of Pebble's owner?
2. What kinds of way are there of being alone?

Chapter 4

1. How can you tell if you are being willed to do something? How would you respond?
2. Can violence ever solve problems?

Chapter 5

1. Discuss some of the things that Wheatear has learned about life since arriving in the Bead Box.
2. "Great oaks from little acorns grow." Can you think of an example of something great that has developed from small beginnings?

Chapter 6

1. "Humans tend to stick together after a shared disaster." Why does this happen, even among strangers? Do you know examples from real life?
2. Who was the real Venerable Bede?

Chapter 7

1. The beads talk about being Chosen. This would mean that they had to leave the life they know. What makes people change the lives they lead? Can you think of an example of someone who has made a big change in their life by choice?

2. What does Verity's name mean?

Chapter 8

1. What do you notice about Wheatear's answer to Verity when she asks him to meet her in the afternoons? (You may need to refer back to Chapter 3.)

2. Amber suffers from bitterness and jealousy. Why are these such dangerous emotions?

Chapter 9

1. What are Wheatear's strengths and weaknesses?

2. How should you prepare for a journey?

Chapter 10

1. This chapter features beads who are 'different' and beads which are exactly the same as each other (e.g. the army). Discuss the advantages of being individual, and of working as a united team. When is each most useful?

2. Discuss the ways in which the Venerable Bead negotiates with Amber. How should power be used wisely?

Chapter 11

1. In what ways has Wheatear's thinking developed since he first arrived in the Bead Box?

2. There are no illustrations in this chapter. Where might you add one? If you like, create an illustration of a particular moment yourself.

Chapter 12

1. The Venerable Bead says, "Everyone should be given a second chance." Do you agree?

2. Wheatear asks the Venerable Bead an important question. If you could question one of the characters in the story, who would it be and what would you ask?

Epilogue

1. Discuss the different viewpoints of the two people and the beads.

2. Who is the girl's mother?

General

1. In order to make the story work, Jane Bower had to give the beads some human attributes. Which did she give the beads, and which did she not?

HOW THIS BOOK CAME TO BE

Thread and Thrum began as a story for the children in my class when I was a primary teacher in Lancashire in the 1980s. Some of my stories had been accepted by BBC's *Play School*, but I wanted to write a full length novel for children – as one of the most delightful aspects of my job was reading to my class at the end of each day. As an art specialist I often used beads; I began to notice the way I chose them, and found myself wondering what life would be like for them.

My parents, Len and Sadie Bower, were both art teachers and trained illustrators, and I asked my father to illustrate the story and my mother to design the cover. While Dad finished the illustrations, sadly

Mum did not manage to complete the cover; other projects and full-time teaching had to come first for both of us, and the story script was set aside – and then forgotten.

Many years later, in 2017, it surfaced in a filing cabinet. By now my mother had died – and my father, aged 97, was registered blind, having gradually lost almost all his sight to macular degeneration. Looking again at his finely detailed illustrations, I felt they should be more widely seen and enjoyed.

I began re-reading the story and making a number of alterations – it was interesting to observe how my language and writing style had changed. As I worked, I recognised that the themes of visual impairment and darkness weave through the story strongly: the beads are deprived of light and full sight, using their senses to lead meaningful and exciting lives, and fulfilment is found by tackling their problems with determination.

These were things I also saw my father doing. He had already sold many of his paintings in aid of the Macular Society, and so now I had the idea of producing this book to raise money for their work also.

So, as a celebration of an artist who, despite losing his sight, has gone on to lead a life full of interest and appreciation, 30% from the sale this book will go to the Macular Society.

I still have the actual beads which inspired the story, though the tin in which they were originally stored was disposed of years ago – largely, of course, because the lid did not fit properly...! I hope children, teachers, and parents alike will all enjoy reading this story, and take from it some inspiration—perhaps that, as Wheatear says, "Great oaks from little acorns grow..."

– Jane Bower, December 2020

GLOSSARY

Bead: A little ball pierced for stringing.

Bead/bede (same derivation): A prayer, e.g. telling beads, saying the rosary. Old English "gebed"—prayer.

Thread and thrum: A combination of good and bad; the good and bad together.

Thrum: 1. A continuous humming or beating sound; 2. Unwanted bits of thread left on the loom after a finished item has been removed.

Venerable Bede: A priest of the monastery of the blessed apostles Peter and Paul; known as the father of English History. Lived circa 672-735AD.

Millefiori (Italian for "thousand flowers"): A technique where many glass rods, each with an intricate pattern, are fused together.

Quercus: A genus of trees containing the oaks.

ABOUT THE AUTHOR

Jane Bower is attempting to be retired, but is too interested in things. She comes from Leeds and trained in Lancaster. Her 40 years' experience with KS1/2 and advisory teaching in art, drama, dance and storytelling also encompassed a 25-year position as an associate lecturer at Cambridge University's Faculty of Education.

She has taught in 615 venues throughout the UK and in India, UAE, and Armenia. She is the author of several books for primary teachers, and for twenty years was a regular writer for monthly educational magazines. She is an elder of the United Reformed Church and a vocal coach to trainee ministers.

Jane also worked as an artist in schools, and her pupils' artwork won several national awards. She has been a professional actor since 1999, and writes and performs her own solo shows and presentations.

Jane's passions include words in any form; choral singing; solo theatre; minute things; and quirky historic buildings, objects, and people.

www.janebower.com

ABOUT THE ILLUSTRATOR

Leonard (Len) Bower had his 100th birthday in June 2020. Born in Leeds, he showed great ability in art, writing and music at an early age. He won a scholarship to train as an illustrator at Leeds College of Art in 1939, but his studies were interrupted by WWII when he joined the RAF as an aircraftsman at Mildenhall, Binbrook and St Athan.

During this time he developed his considerable skills in illustration (using it to teach other aircraftsmen about the structure of planes) and in playing the clarinet and piano to an extremely high standard. His playing was constantly sought after in numerous venues both during and after the war. Back in Leeds he won first prize in the Melody Maker music awards, playing his own composition with his band Four Star Quartet. He was head-hunted by agents in London and could have had a professional career in music – but during the war his natural abilities as a teacher had caught the eye of a commanding officer, and he found his true vocation. He was called back to St Athan, this time as an instructor. After completing his studies at Leeds

College of Art, where he met his wife Sadie (who also became a renowned art teacher in Leeds), he became Head of Art at Batley Grammar School, and then a senior lecturer in Art Education back at Leeds College of Art.

Because Len chose to become a teacher rather than an illustrator, he never had any work published until Jane asked him to illustrate *Thread and Thrum* – although he produced a constant stream of highly professional artwork, posters and visual aids for all kinds of occasions, mainly church-related.

Around the age of 94 he gradually lost his sight to macular degeneration.

Apart from his six years in the RAF he has lived in Leeds all his life. His witty, humorous war diaries and poignant memoirs inspired his daughter Jane Bower to write and perform her solo show *Daddy's Diaries* about his remarkable war years. The show features his illustrations and original recordings of his playing. You can learn more about Len by watching the show here:

www.tinyurl.com/daddysdiaries

Author Jane with her father, illustrator Len

Epic Tales

If you love stories,
why not invite an Epic Storyteller
into your school?

Your teachers will love it too – just let them know that storytelling has been scientifically proven to help children learn faster and more effectively than anything else. They can find some of this proof at **epictales.co.uk/proof**

Oh, and the best part? They can start within seconds by visiting **epictales.co.uk/stories** and using our storytelling videos in class.

And the *better* best part? It's fun!

Ask your teachers to let us know you found this message in *Thread and Thrum*, and we'll make sure we do something extra special for your class (and something your school's finance officer will like too).

We hope to hear *your* story soon!

Epic Ink

Stories you'll carry with you

@EpicTalesST

www.epictales.co.uk

Lightning Source UK Ltd.
Milton Keynes UK
UKHW021026171220
375366UK00007B/237